Romantic Blue

ISBN: 9781729160749

Contents

A Man for Christmas

Love Letter Secrets

Love Letters from a Lonely Man

Love Letters from Space

Can't Help Falling

Love Letters to His Ex

A Man for Christmas

I guess you could call me pretty useless. I got divorced because I realized that I liked men. I wanted to be free to find a man, and not to have to live a lie anymore. But somehow things didn't work out as I had planned.

I found myself sitting in gay bars and wishing that someone would notice me. I hadn't a clue how to go about initiating a conversation, let alone picking up a man; I had no idea if I held any kind of appeal for anyone. I soon found out that, come closing time, some men saw the world through beer goggles and some of them found me attractive enough to take home. Sadly, they never found me attractive enough to make any kind of connection that could go the distance. I was just about regretting ever having gotten divorced when my parents decided that they wanted to retire down by the seaside and that they would gift their business and the house to me.

And so I found myself back in the same small, off the beaten tack, town that I had started life in. Well, at least there would be no rejection here because there simply were no gay men in town, period. The store I had inherited was so far back in the twentieth century that it wasn't even funny, and I soon realized that there was nothing I could do to change it. The customers wanted it exactly the way it was. My only thrill came when some big farmer would come into the store looking for a pair of new underpants. As I showed him what we had in size forty four inch scants, I would secretly fantasize about what he was going to pour into those scants. We're all allowed to dream, aren't we?

I had been away from town far too long to have any kind of real connection with my peers. We stopped and said hello when we saw each other, but that was pretty much it. I sat alone each evening, moping about how lonely I was. Red wine proved to be a faithful friend. It wasn't healthy, that's for sure.

'What are you doing for Christmas?' Gareth surprised me by asking me one day when he came into the store.

'Nothing.' I said.

'We can't have that.' he replied. 'You're coming round to our place.'

'I don't want to put you out.' I said.

I was on the same cricket team as his younger brother back in high school. That was about our only connection, so I was a little surprised by his invitation. But then again, folks in really small towns march to a different drum; everyone is a potential friend. Perhaps I had been so set on finding a man that I had forgotten about ordinary friendships. His generosity made me feel guilty about how little of myself I had given to others since moving back here.

'Nonsense. It's no bother. It will just be me and Diana, and Diana's brother Tom. We'll have a barbecue, like we always do, so there's no fuss with cooking and decorating, and all that stuff.'

'Are you sure?' I asked.

'Absolutely.' he said. 'I think you'll like Tom.'

I found myself wondering what he meant by that. Was there something I didn't know? Why would I like Tom? Oh well, it was too late; I was spending Christmas with Gareth and his family, whether I liked it or not. If you're reading this in the northern hemisphere it might seem a little odd to have a barbecue at Christmas, but while you guys are into your snow, candles, wreaths, lights and being all cosy indoors, down in the southern hemisphere we're baking in the heat. You can't quite get into the full holiday-mood thing of Christmas when the sun is shining and the sweat is pouring off you. A barbecue is an ideal no-fuss alternative to a huge Christmas meal, and as long as I am not the one standing over the hot fire I'm happy.

Gareth is a big-boned blonde hunk of beef. He is a banana farmer and lives his life in comfortable cotton shirts, well-worn rugby shorts and boots. He has this unfortunate habit of always tucking his shirt into his shorts whenever he is in the store, and I am unable to look away. The shirt goes down and the shorts come up and I see the outline of something I really don't want to see but, like I said, I can't look away.

I'm probably painting a rather unfavourable picture of myself, aren't I? It's just that I get so lonely, and so...you know; I surely don't have to spell it out. It had been such a long time since I had been with a man that I was beginning to wonder if I really was gay. Perhaps it was just early onset midlife crisis? Most sensible men would have gone out on the down low a time or two instead of throwing their marriage away.

I always feel real guilty when I think about Carly. You see, I loved her; love her still. It wasn't as if I was unable to function, or anything like that. It's just that I felt terribly guilty for thinking about men. And when I started to think about men when we were making love I knew that I had to be brave and do something about those feelings. Don't ask me where they came from. I had never experimented with another guy when I was younger, the way some straight guys do.

The moment I laid eyes on Tom I knew I was in trouble. I realized that I had seen him before; he was the captain of a visiting rugby team that had played in a match I had watched. If I'm honest, I don't have that much interest in rugby; I think you know why I watch the game. There's something about seeing a group of masculine, sweaty men chasing around a field and bending over, often, that appeals to me. In my dreams the guys would hug and kiss at the end of a match and then take their pent-up feelings into the showers. I'm sure I could get a job as a director of a certain kind of movie! I've got to stop this; I promised myself that I would keep this clean.

'Vince, this is Tom. Tom, Vince.' Gareth introduced us.

'Hi.' he said in this deep, sexy voice as he stuck out his hand.

Electricity arced through me as our palms met. I wondered if Gareth and Tom were aware of what was happening to me. I barely managed a greeting as I looked into his warm brown eyes and practically melted. He flashed me a smile then, and I felt weak-kneed.

'Gareth tells me you run a general dealers store.' Tom said.

'I do.'

'I'm in the same line of work, over in Harriston.'

'My rival.' I said.

'Hardly.' Tom replied. 'I don't think most folk in Harriston have ever been over this way and probably the same goes for people living here; I guess they don't get out much. But you escaped, for a while, didn't you.'

'Yes. My parents decided to retire and they handed the business over to me. I was at a loose end so I came back.'

'Do you regret coming back?' he asked.

'The only problem I have with living here is the loneliness.' I replied.

'A good-looking guy like you?' Tom said. 'Surely the ladies must be falling at your feet.'

'A little bird told me that Vince isn't into the ladies.' Gareth said. 'At least, not anymore.'

'Oh!'

Tom's nostrils flared and his eyes widened. I wondered if he was grossed out but no, there was something about the way he quickly licked his lips that told me something else was going on. Now suddenly I understood why Gareth had said I would like Tom.

'Well, that's two things we have in common.' Tom rasped.

Oh my word! I wanted to rip his clothes off right then and there. But that would have been stupid. I had not encountered a single gay man since moving back here and it would not be worth throwing away the possibility of making a friend, if not finding a lover. He grinned at me and I grinned at him. Already I was tripping down love lane into the future. The idea of waking up next to this gorgeous rugger-bugger each morning was enough to motivate me to get through whatever life decided to throw at me. Loneliness was already floating out of the window as I thought about a future with Tom in it.

'I told you that you would like Tom.' Gareth said.

'Are you matchmaking again?' Diana asked Gareth as she came into the room.

'Has he had many offers?' I asked her.

'No. Gareth's matchmaking skills have not been all that great. He tried to pair him off with a couple of straight guys, and a gay guy who was already paired up with someone.'

'Oh.'

'Come on, let's get this barbecue started.' Gareth said.

He and Tom went off to attend to the barbecue while I went into the kitchen to help Diana with the salads.

'I can see that the sparks are flying between you two.' Diana said.

'Do you think?'

'Oh yes, he is certainly interested.'

'I've not had much experience with relationships with guys.' I told her.

'Yes. I heard that you used to be married. She wasn't a local girl, was she?'

'Carly? No. I met her after I left. I loved that woman...I still do; it's just that I started developing feelings towards guys.'

'Did you ask for the divorce?' Diana asked me.

'Yes.'

'That was brave of you. Some guys just go out and get what they want on the side.'

'I didn't want to be one of those guys.'

'Tom wasn't as honest as you are.' she said. 'It was a huge scandal when Laura caught him in bed with another guy. She had gone off to look after her sick Mom but when her Mom recovered, sooner than expected, she hurried home to be with her darling husband. Only she found him underneath another guy. She walked out, instantly, and only went back to fetch her clothes. The gossip was all over town in a matter of minutes. Tom told me that he realized then that he had to come out. He could never go back in the closet.'

My head was reeling at the news. He had been found underneath a guy! That answered something I had been curious about since he announced that we had something in common. I knew so little about gay life but one thing I did know was that I wanted a versatile man. I wanted to give, and take, love and I still could not believe how so many men were so rigid about what they would, and wouldn't do, in bed. I didn't see the point in being gay if you didn't want to explore a man's body in every way it can be explored.

I was starting to get all hot and bothered again. It was time to cool down.

'The pool looks inviting.' I said as I gazed out of the window.

'You did bring your cozzie, didn't you?' Diana asked.

'Yes.' I replied. 'Gareth made sure that I remembered.'

'It will probably be at least an hour before we are ready to eat. You might want to have a little dip in the pool.'

I sure did. I went and got changed into my Budgy Smugglers and went out to the pool. I noticed Tom's eyes drink in every inch of my body and I felt more thrilled than I had ever been in my life. A man was looking at me with unbridled lust and desire! The self-same man that I had already started building my dreams around was looking at me the way I wanted a man to look at me, right from the start; I didn't want to just be looked at like this when men were tanked up on beers and the bar was about to close. His eyes caressed my face, and then roamed over my torso, across my hairy chest and down my belly before settling on the budge in my swimwear. I had felt a little self-conscious as I poured myself into that little scrap of fabric, and had almost chickened out and changed into a pair of more modest swim shorts, but I was mighty glad that I hadn't.

'Down boy!' Gareth teased his brother-in-law.

I was impressed at how at ease Gareth was with Tom. Not having had any siblings, I have no way of knowing what kind of relationship I might have had with a brother, or brother-in-law. Somehow I don't think we would have got on so easily. In our family being a man meant liking women only. My parents had been thoroughly confused when Carly had told them that the reason we were getting divorced was because I wanted to be with a man. My mother told me that she had had a hard time convincing my Dad not to give the house and business to Carly. It was only the fact that she had started dating again so soon after the divorce that had swayed his mind. Dad is very traditional and probably found it hard to understand her actions. However, I knew what Carly was trying to do: I had heard the expression that the best way to get over a man was to get under another, and I'm sure she had too.

I dived into the pool and began to swim laps. As I swam back and forth I was aware that Tom was watching me and I felt a delicious thrill that quickened my pulse. When I got out of the pool I pretended that I had water in my eyes and I stood there letting Tom get an eyeful if he wanted to. I had always been second best in the bars I had visited but here I was king. On Barry's banana farm I was the king banana! Oh he looked alright, hard and long and I have to resist making a crude joke as I write this. Sorry, but do you know what it's like standing there with a pair of wet Budgy Smugglers clinging to you every contour, and knowing that someone is looking you over, and approving of what they see? I felt like breaking out in a Cece Peniston song!

I went and got changed back into my clothes, having only just managed to contain my excitement. I felt like a completely different man; somehow the physicality had come to the fore and I saw no reason not to celebrate it. I was alive, in reasonable shape and I had some sweet, sensitive ruggedly good-looking hunk interested in me! When I went into the kitchen Tom was in there with Diana. It was obvious that they were talking about me as they quickly changed the subject as I walked into the room. I was hooked on all the attention!

'Did you enjoy your swim?' Tom asked.

'Yes, very much.' I told him.

'I don't think it's fair, you just about giving me a heart attack on Christmas Day.' he said.

I squirmed and grinned. He suddenly took me into his arms briefly and kissed my forehead.

'Take that out to Gareth, will you?' Diana said to me as she pressed a bowl of shrimp into my hands.

I was in a daze as I walked out of that kitchen. Something was happening to me, after all this time. It felt as though I had waited a lifetime for this moment. You and me Cece, you and me! Finally! Oh, I wanted to bust some moves!

'So, been around the block have you while you lived in town?' Gareth asked me.

'No!' I said. 'If you must know, I'm not very experienced.'

'Good.' he said. 'Tom is a real gentle, sensitive kind of guy. He's had his fingers burned a few times and he could do with making a good friend.'

'I was kinda hoping for more than friends.' I said.

'Believe me, you're going to get more than friends.' Gareth replied. 'The men on Diana's side of the family are rather...shall we say gifted?'

I was shocked and could do nothing but grin.

'Now, if you had gone for me you would have been totally disappointed.' he said.

Gareth suddenly pulled his rugby shorts, and undies, away from his belly and I caught sight of the little worm in question. I didn't know what to think or say. So what I had been seeing, every time he tucked in his shirt, and pulled up his shorts, was literally all bollocks. Fortunately I was saved by Diana and Tom coming outside just then. Gareth had just flashed his willy at me but he was as calm as a cucumber as he kissed his wife on the cheek. Somehow I knew that what I had just witnessed was something we would never talk about again and was not even something that I could share with Tom. Perhaps Gareth just wanted a bit of the crazy magic that was floating around Tom and me.

The food was wonderful and the big, bold Margaret River red was even more so.

'Have you ever been out west, Vince?' Tom asked.

'No, never. It's on my wish list.'

'Me too.' he said. 'Wouldn't it be wonderful to do a road trip some day?'

Was that "wouldn't it be wonderful to do a road trip with me" or just wouldn't it be wonderful to do a road trip?

'When do you go back to work, Vince?' Gareth asked.

'Two weeks from now.' I said. 'Bill will be looking after the store for me.'

'Well, Tom is off for a couple of weeks too. I suggest you set off tomorrow.'

I gulped. Surely that wasn't possible. Okay, so I got the feeling that Tom liked me, but surely he didn't like me enough to spend two weeks on the road with me.

'I want to get to know Tom.' I said. 'I don't think it would be wise for us to go off on a road trip together when we've only just met.'

'You're probably right.' Tom said. 'But, my word, I'm tempted. This is the only real holiday time that I get. The idea of just you and me, and the open road seems very appealing.'

'Be brave.' Gareth said. 'You will have the perfect excuse to get along.'

The two weeks that I was going to have away from the store was pretty much the only holiday time that I too had. Suddenly Gareth's words seemed very appropriate. Nothing ventured, nothing gained, and all that.

'My little worm says you should go.' Gareth said.

'What!' Diana asked.

I wanted to laugh out loud. I was really starting to warm to Gareth.

'Do you think we should?' I asked Tom.

'Yes. Let's do this.' he said. 'We can reign in our ambition. We don't have to go too far, but let's head west and see a little of the countryside. If we aren't getting along we can always turn around and come home.'

'That sounds like a good plan.' Diana said.

Incredibly, it was that easy. Gareth got a map out and the four of us planned a route for Tom and me to take. I could not remember when last I had been this excited. Afterwards Tom had a swim and I saw that what Gareth had told me was true.

'Pretty impressive, huh?' Gareth said as he came up beside me.

'What is?' Diana asked.

'The size of the country.' Gareth replied. 'You can travel for days and days and it hardly seems like you've reached anywhere.'

The four of us watched a movie together and then had an early supper. Afterwards Tom and I headed to our respective homes to pack. I was on cloud nine as I threw a few clothes into a suitcase. Tom had already told me that he didn't care much for clothes and I realized that he was a man after my own heart. I called Billy and told him that I would be away for a while and that it would just be tough if he needed me. I think he was a little astonished by this change in me, but glad to have a chance to prove himself.

Tom picked me up early the next morning and I was glad to note that he was punctual. That was one more thing I could cross of my worry list.

'You know that we can change our mind about the route.' he said to me. 'We don't have to follow the one we mapped out with Gareth and Diana.'

'I'm happy to go wherever you want to.' I told him. 'Gareth is quite some guy, isn't he?'

'I've never seen him like that with a guy before.' Tom said. 'If I didn't know that he was straight I would almost say that he was flirting with you.'

'Get outta here!'

He placed his hand on my knee and gave it a little squeeze.

'I've got a good feeling about this trip.' he said.

'Me too.'

The miles flew by. I was relaxed, happy seeing countryside I had never seen before. What more could I ask for? Well, that would have to wait. The anticipation delighted and excited me and I just could not stop smiling.

'You've not stopped grinning since we started this trip.' Tom said to me.

'I've never done anything this spontaneous before.' I said.

'Me neither.' he said. 'I er...I used to be married once and then this guy started to come on to me. I treated it as a bit of a joke at first. You know, how often are you going to get a man in a small town telling you he wants to take your pants off. I was shocked by the stuff he said to me, but I guess there was something in me that he saw. And then, one day, my wife went off to take care of her sick mother. It was a moment of weakness; I let him into my bed. She chose just that moment to return early. Boy, did the shit hit the fan! I was divorced before I knew it.'

'What happened to the guy?' I asked.

'He lost interest.' Tom said, in this sad little voice. 'He told me that he was only into married men. That was my first big disappointment. Some while later I met a guy and I thought we were getting along real great. It turned out that he and his wife were only separated, not divorced, as he had told me, and that they were supposed to be working their way through their differences. She came home, ready to forgive him, and he decided that gay sex was an itch that he had needed to scratch, but that he had now been there, and done that.'

'Oh.'

'I'm not very experienced.' he said.

'Me neither.' I told him. 'I was married too. I came to realize that I liked guys and decided that I would not live a lie so I asked my wife for a divorce. It was really hard, on both of us. I had never even been with a man at that stage; she couldn't understand how I could throw away a marriage for something I hadn't even tried.'

'I don't think I would have been that brave.' he said.

'Well, I wanted to be free to find a man.' I said. 'Somehow things didn't go according to plan. I had no idea how to go about meeting men so I would go to gay bars. I'd sit there all evening, hoping that someone would notice me. Men only noticed me at closing time and in the morning didn't seem that keen on having me around.'

'Ouch!' Tom said.

'Ouch indeed. It didn't do my ego any good.' I told him. 'Just so you know, I've been bruised. I've never been with a guy who liked me for who I was. I was always just a convenience, the substitute for the one that got away.'

'You're not going to go all Garland on me?' he asked.

I smiled, glad that we had something else in common.

'Just so you know,' Tom said 'we can take this as slow as you want to. We don't have to do anything you don't want to.'

'Thanks.' I said. 'But I wish that I hadn't seen you in your Speedos. Gareth told me that you were a big boy.'

'He said that?'

'He did indeed.'

'I didn't think that straight guys noticed such things.' Tom said.

'They've got eyes, just like everyone else.' I chuckled.

I relaxed deeper and deeper into being with Tom. We stopped at a small country hotel and had lunch. We had to resist the temptation to just have a couple of beers with our lunch and check into the hotel, but Tom felt that we deserved something a little more salubrious. I had to agree. Also, I didn't like the way the way the hotel owner was looking at us. Either he was hot for a little homo love sauce, or he disapproved of the way Tom and I gazed into each other's eyes. I was too inexperienced to tell which it was. Either way, I knew that I would not be totally relaxed until we had started back on the road.

We hit the road again and promised ourselves that when we did have an ice cold beer it wouldn't even touch sides as it sloshed down to our bellies. I felt silly and happy and on the edge of something monumental. I drove and Tom gazed out the window and told me little snippets about his life. Once more we chewed up the miles without even realizing it; it definitely is true that time flies when you're having fun. As the shadows started to lengthen we saw a small country hotel; we just instinctively knew it was what we were looking for.

'It looks pretty romantic.' Tom said.

'And pricey.'

'Who care about money on a night like this?' Tom asked. 'Besides, I'm going to sell my store and be your wife; you will have to take care of me.'

I laughed, drunk with happiness and possibility. The owners of the hotel were a very sweet lesbian couple and we were made to feel right at home. It didn't take us long to notice that we weren't the only gay couple in the place.

'I suppose I'm going to lose you to some tall, dark stranger.' I said to Tom.

'Fat chance.' he replied as he slipped his hand into mine.

It was the first time that I had ever held hands with a man. My heart raced and I felt breathless and almost delirious. I turned to him and planted a quick kiss on his cheek as we walked along to our room.

'Someone might see us!' he hissed.

'I wish they would!' I said. 'I want the whole world to know just how happy I am right at this minute.'

Tom took me into his arms the moment we closed the door. We kissed, really kissed and I knew then that he was the one for me. It might sound silly, and soppy, but I knew that there could be no other. This was my soul mate and it felt as though I had loved him even before I knew him.

'I think maybe we should take a walk.' Tom said. 'If I don't stop kissing you we might end up doing something we might not want to do just yet.'

'We can take a walk,' I said 'or we can...you know...'

'Let's take a walk. The anticipation is most delightful.'

We walked through the hotel grounds and sat by a little pond, listening to bird calls and watching darkness creep in. The heat of the day was spent and a delightfully cool breeze stirred the vegetation around the pond. It seemed the most perfect way to spend some time, better even than what we could have been doing if we had stayed in the room. Another gay couple came and sat on the bench next to us and we watched as they held hands and whispered sweet nothings to each other.

'How long have you guys been together?' one of the pair asked.

'Since this morning.' Tom replied.

'Wow! That's exciting.' he said. 'But you look like you've been together longer than that.'

'Perhaps we were meant to be.' I said.

'You might be right.' he said. 'We've been together twelve years and I don't regret a single moment.'

I was jealous that they had had all that time together. Hopefully Tom and I would be able to look back one day and say that we had had twelve years together. He squeezed my hand and kissed it.

'I want at least twelve years with you.' he whispered.

'I don't think you will ever be able to get rid of me.' I said.

That evening we had full, traditional Christmas fare for supper and we enjoyed it immensely. Carol and Megan came out and worked the tables, ensuring that everyone felt welcome. We had stumbled upon the hotel by chance but it would seem that many of the other guests were regulars. The other people in the dining room were very friendly and it turned out to be a memorable occasion, and not just because it was the first evening I had spent with Tom.

Later, in bed, Tom proved to be as versatile as I had hoped. Everything we did, we did in love. That first voyage of discovery was a mind-blower and I will treasure the memory for the rest of my days. It was precisely what I had been looking for. As Tom and I cuddled that night and started to drift into sleep I wished that we could do it all again. And that's when I realized that we could; if we were prepared to commit to each other we could have this little bit of paradise right here on earth.

That was six years ago. We were just meant to be. I thought that I was getting a man for Christmas, but it turned out that I was being given a much more precious gift.

***

Love Letter Secrets

Dear Marti

This is crazy. Stuff like this is not supposed to happen. Or, if it does, it happens the other way around. Married men sneak about and visit their boyfriends; you don't get gay guys suddenly having their heads turned by a woman.

I've never been with a woman; I can't even say that I have ever really thought about a woman in a romantic or sexual way before now, not really. Even since my hormones kicked in, I've thought about big, hairy brutes. You've seen Geoff, my ex. And yet now...I'm not so sure any more. I don't understand what is happening to me. I feel I ought to knock this thing on the head, so to speak. Perhaps you can tell me what the allure is? What magic spell do you possess that gets me thinking about you several times a day? Could it be your flaming locks and smoky green eyes? Or the way you look so deeply into my eyes that I feel you are boring right into my soul?

I know it was just a bit of harmless flirting at first. You laughed when I told you that I was gay, you said it was the most pathetic excuse you had ever heard for turning a girl down. When it dawned on you that I really was gay, you just smiled and told me that you would turn me straight. I just laughed at that. As if! But hell, I'm so confused right now. This is not where I thought I would be at this stage of my life; I thought that I had shaken off all the angst of years ago, and had worked through all of my insecurities.

That kiss was meant to be a peck on the cheek, just a nice friendly peck on the cheek. But then your perfume overpowered me; your hands guided my face to yours and aligned our lips. I was shocked by how much it excited me. You see, I love to hold a man's face in my hands, to feel his stubble and kiss his juicy lips. It's a clash of equals, of beef on beef. Your face felt so delicate in my hands, your skin so smooth, and I know you were looking to me to take the lead. Though our kiss lasted but a few seconds I can't get it out of my mind. I guess this is how a straight man would feel if he had a moment of madness with another guy, except he would be seeking to get rid of the memory. I somehow can't let it go.

You need to know that I would always be a disappointment to you, should anything ever happen between us. I would always be looking at this guy, that ass, those legs...the list goes on and on. I'm very physical and easily led. I'd probably always be sneaking away, back to my roots. You know, it has taken me ages to feel comfortable in my own skin, to be able to look anyone in the eye and say that I am proud to be gay. And then you come along!

Last night I went to a gay bar, hoping to get lucky. I wanted to put some distance between us. But I was sitting there like a zombie, not in the mood to chat to anyone, let alone chat them up. And then in walks Geoff with some gorgeous hunk, and that just put a dampener on everything. I left immediately and he followed me out. And then...in the car park he pulled me into his arms and kissed me. All the emotions that I had suppressed after our break up surfaced and I was overcome. And then he was apologizing, telling me that he shouldn't have kissed me but that I was looking so sad he just couldn't help it. I had to get away from him then because I yearned for him with every atom of my being. I would have let him bend me over the hood of a vehicle right in that car park, that's how deep my need of him was.

Oh hell! Why am I telling you this? I'm just so mixed up and confused right now, and I don't know what to think of anything anymore. Tell me to fuck off, to stay out of your life. Tell me that I'm spineless and need to grow up.

Yours

Eric

Dear Eric

You're confused! I don't know what that makes me. My head was all over the place when I read your letter.

I didn't think I'd ever hear from you. I was beating up on myself or taking things too far, with the kiss. And then you tell me how you keep thinking about our kiss and I start to feel this hope bubbling up inside. And then you end your letter by telling me how you kissed your ex, and how you would have spread your legs for him right there in the car park if he had asked you to.

I don't know what to say, or what to advise. If I was rational, I would say we should let sleeping dogs lie. But every time I see your handsome face, and the twinkle in your deep-blue eyes, my heart springs alive. I know then what I have always suspected: that I have been sleepwalking through life. I feel so excited upon seeing you that I worry that the whole world can see my beating crotch. I feel damp, just thinking about you. Oh Eric, life is so unfair. You want a stubbled face to hold in your hands, and so do I.

A friend of mine is dating a married man and I get so bored listening to all her moaning. You made that bed, I feel like screaming, and yet here I am in the same boat. I'll be perfectly honest; my dream would be to have you exclusively to myself. I wouldn't want to be waiting outside a bathroom, wondering why you were taking so long. I wouldn't want to see you looking at a clump of bushes and thinking what a good trysting place it would make. I know it would never work between us but, my goodness, how I would want it to. You see, I would spread my legs for you anywhere, anytime; that's how bad I've got it. I'm shocked that I even think these thoughts, let alone write them down. I was always so conventional, a real good girl until I fell for a certain macho slut.

If I was sensible I would say that we should not write to each other, and should not see each other again, but already I long to see your ruggedly-handsome face, to see your sweet tush in your faded jeans. Oh! I really should not have written that. I'm going to end before I put my foot in my mouth.

Yours

Marti

Dear Marti

I didn't know that you felt that strongly about me that you would be prepared to get all raunchy in public!

Something's happened, and I feel awful. Geoff came to see me, to apologize for kissing me and we ended up making love. I was on such an emotional high. I don't think I have ever enjoyed carnality as much as I did that evening. It was as if the past six months had ceased to exist. And then, when it was over, I asked him where that left us. He was confused about why I thought there was an 'us'. Can you believe that! It turns out that he is still seeing gorgeous guy, the one with the muscles, the perfect teeth and trendy haircut.

I felt about two inches tall when Geoff left and cried myself to sleep. I know now that I could never do that to you, and have to ensure that we never are an item. I'm damaged goods and I'm no use to you. Perhaps I'll meet a guy who will take pity on me. Or perhaps I'll just hang out in darkrooms and saunas, hoping that someone might want a quick fumble. I sound pathetic don't I? I know that I need to get a grip. I need to go back to my gym and work out a little, and try to get my confidence back. I've felt low for so long now.

Forgive me for burdening you with all this crap, but I feel like I can really talk to you. There's this guy at the office, a real sweet, chubby guy and I know that he is keen on me, and would like to get to know me, but he really is not my kind. It's not so much because he is chubby but because he is too passive. If I wanted someone I would let them know about, it whereas he is just wishing that I would suddenly develop an interest in him. He hardly can say boo to a goose. Oh, I'm being cruel, aren't I. Why am I thinking about him? Any romance between us would be bound to fizzle out after five minutes. He has really smooth skin, and doesn't even look like he shaves.

I thought I was writing to say goodbye, now I'm not so sure. I think I might be even more mixed up than that bastard Geoff. How I hate him so much right now!

Yours

Eric

Dear Eric

It sounds like I have become a gay agony aunt or, more correctly, an agony aunt for gay men. How did that happen? Especially since I want to jump your bones!

I had no idea that you were so emotional and romantic. It just makes me want you more. My word, I'd fuck your brains out given half the chance. I offer no apologies for saying that; it's how I feel. I'm sure you must have drooled over a gay man or three in your time.

I don't know what to say about Geoff. I don't know what to say about anything, except please don't say goodbye.

Yours

Marti

Dear Marti

I'm sorry for dumping on you with all the emotional stuff. I was in a really bad place when I wrote that letter. I feel much better now. I've spoken with Geoff and we've agreed that we can't be friends. There's too much history between us for that to work, and not enough spark to be lovers again; well, that's how he feels, not me. I loved that man the moment I laid eyes on him. I don't think he was even aware of my existence and I made sure that he noticed me. It was hard working wooing that man, but I won him in the end. And look where that got me. I guess there's a moral in there somewhere: don't go chasing after handsome devils; they will only break your heart.

And how is this for a kick in the teeth: the other day, as I was leaving work, I saw gorgeous guy's twin get out of his vehicle and walk straight up to Carl, the chubby guy I told you about. I must have turned twenty shades of green. So Carl wasn't trying to seduce me, nor was he waiting for me to make a move. He already had a relationship going with one seriously hot stud.

I guess you could say that I'm feeling pretty low right now. The stuff you said in your last letter lifted my spirits somewhat. Thank you.

Yours

Eric

Dear Marti

I could not believe it when I came out of the office and saw you waiting for me. You insisted that we do drinks. Well, we did drinks, and dinner and a whole lot more besides. I honestly never thought that I would ever go with a woman! My head is still in a spin.

I don't know how to explain how I feel. It was way nicer than I thought it would be and I don't know how to explain that, given that you're not muscular and hairy, and that you don't have a ruddy great big cock. I made love to a woman! Me! Who would ever have thought it?

I know you were just being kind when you said you didn't expect me to feel anything for you. That's not how you truly feel. I could see it in your eyes; I heard that gag in your voice as you tripped into ecstasy. Man, did that make me feel proud! Oh, don't let me swagger.

I used to wonder about all those men who describe themselves as bi curious. I guess I've joined their ranks. I just can't stop thinking about it, and I feel I want to do it again. Is that crazy?

Yours

Eric

Dear Eric

I don't think it's crazy. What it is, is an ego boost for me. You slept with me and want to do it again, instead of running for the hills. I want to make love with you again. You were a very generous, and very gifted, lover.

I haven't told anyone about us, because it seems so crazy. I know all my girlfriends would ask what kind of crazy fool would sleep with a gay guy. One of my friends recently discovered that her husband was cheating on her with a guy. She almost had a breakdown. She just could not accept that her big, masculine husband was driving nearly forty miles to go visit this effeminate little guy living in a one-horse town. She said that the guy was way prettier than she was, and that really grossed her out. She had tried to get hold of her husband at work one day, and they told her that he had taken the day off, as he always did on a Tuesday and the shit hit the fan. When she asked him what he wanted out of life he replied that he wanted both of them. Weird huh? Or perhaps not quite so weird, for you? She gave him an ultimatum and he chose his boyfriend. She can't live that down.

Work is getting a little bit hectic. One of my colleagues quit when she won some money on the lottery. One day she was at work, the next she was planning on jetting around the world. The boss has promised to recruit someone new, but he is such a mean bastard that I wonder if he will. If we take up the slack he will probably just rub his hands in glee.

Eric, please don't feel pressurized, but if you ever want to make out with a woman again promise that I'll be first in line.

Yours

Marti

Dear Marti

I can't believe I've done it again. A part of me wants to apologize, and tell you that I will stay away from you, so that I don't break your heart. Another part of me wants to shout it from the rooftops.

I once made love to a married man - he said it was his first time ever - and he just watched me doing all the things I did to him. And then he surprised me by rolling over onto his belly. Afterwards, he told me that it was the most amazing experience of his life but one that he would never repeat. I felt like that the first time I was with you, but now I'm beginning to wonder about the validity of labels. Yes, I am a gay man but my head sure is turned by one very pretty lady.

Could you handle me being the way I am? Could you handle it if we were out together somewhere and some gorgeous man walks by and my neck cranes around? What would you say if we were watching a movie and you knew we were both drooling over the same guy? Or if I called a man's name in my sleep? No, this could never work, could it? Spare yourself the heartache and find a man who is one hundred percent straight.

Yours

Eric

Dear Eric

One hundred percent straight? Do such men even exist? Judging from the things that you have told me, I doubt it. I'm in far too deep now to let you go. I accept you with all of your faults, and your slutty bum. Sorry, just had to throw that in there.

Seriously though, would I be the first woman to be in love with a gay man? No. Would I give you the freedom you need? Yes. Why, you ask. Why not? You have given me something so rare, so precious. All other men I have known fade into insignificance. Please don't think that I am stereotyping when I say that you are incredibly sensitive and intuitive. And you are an amazing lover! I know that this is a rocky path that I am about to walk down but I would not have it any other way. Just be there, for as long as you can. Keep coming back for more hot sex, for as long as you want. I don't care, think about him while you're doing me; just do me!

I've not felt this elated for many a year! I know that I should feel stupid and humiliated - according to conventional wisdom - but I don't. I feel alive. And that's all we can ask for.

Love

Marti

Dear Marti

I have something to tell you, because I know that you would want me to be honest with you. Geoff came to visit me recently. He's been going through a hard time with gorgeous guy. You see, gorgeous guy is too gorgeous for his own good; everyone wants him and he finds it difficult to say no. I felt so incredibly emotional, and vulnerable, in Geoff's presence. And when he started to rub my wrist, the way he used to do when he wanted sex, I couldn't say no.

Now I feel cheap and dirty. He doesn't want me; even though he was in my arms it was as if I was making love to a stranger. He could never give himself to me with one hundred percent commitment, even if we were to get back together again. Why on earth would you want to be with someone who could never give that to you?

You're smart, and funny, with a wise head on your shoulders. Go out there and find your dream man. In amongst all the heart-breakers, and time-wasters, there must be the perfect man for you. You deserve the best; you know you do.

Love

Eric

Dear Marti

I had no idea that you would come around as soon as you got my letter! That's three times now I've made love to a woman. This is starting to become something of a habit.

I told a good fried about us and he thinks that we are both going to end up getting hurt. We were lovers years ago, and the end of our relationship was painful for both of us. He thought that the gay thing was just a phase. He got married and started a family. And then, one night while sitting in a bar, a guy looked at him and saw into the depths of him. It wasn't long before his wife found out about the affair and his life started to unravel. He is still with his boyfriend and I will always think of Adam as the one that got away.

It's hard not to take Adam's advice; he's been there and done that. The only difference is that I don't think that I'm straight. I just happen to have this thing going on with a woman. Man, is that crazy, or what! I'm saying that, but I'm sitting here and thinking how smooth your skin is, how wonderful it is to hear you moan like that.

Where the hell is this thing going? I want to be brave and throw caution to the wind, and say 'let's explore'. But is that fair to either of us? What if it is just some crazy infatuation, just late onset curiosity? I've been looking at job offers out of state. There's this part of me that wants to flee, and put some difference between us. I tell you that only because we have always been honest with each other, and I am a coward.

Love

Eric

Dear Eric

Please stop looking at those job offers! Running away is not going to solve anything. Being with you feels perfect to me. I know you find it a little confusing, but running away? You're braver than that. You have to look me in the eye and tell me that you don't want to see me again. You know that I would walk away from this, if you wanted me to.

I saw an ex-boyfriend of mine recently. He told me that he had heard that I was dating a gay guy; a mutual friend saw us out together. I think his ego was bruised, and yet he was also mighty curious. He wanted to know about the sex and I told him that he ought to know me better than to expect me to discuss that. He said that he felt sorry for me. How could he? I felt sorry for myself when I was with him, always having to hear his lies and excuses. I used to feel so lonely when he would roll off me after two minutes and start snoring.

You know what I think? I think we should not take advice from anyone. If you were a straight man who had fallen in love with a gay man I bet everyone would tell you to go for it. This is our situation: we got ourselves into it and we will find a way to deal with it. Either we will be brave, and see where this leads, or we will say goodbye. You might then be happy, chasing after men in bars and clubs, but know that I will be sitting home alone and weeping my eyes out. I love you Eric Vincent de Burgh, and I will not settle for anything less.

Love

Marti

Dear Marti

Geoff came to see me again. He told me that he had broken up with gorgeous guy. He said that he felt much too insecure being with him. He also apologized for making me feel that way when we were together. He then asked me if there was any way that we could be together. I told him that there wasn't, that I was in love with someone else. He wanted to know who the lucky guy was. You should have seen his face when I told him that it was a woman.

He gave me the usual advice that it couldn't, and wouldn't, work. And all the time he was telling me this I felt serenely peaceful. You see, I knew then that it would work. I was giving up the chance to be reunited with the only man, apart from Adam, that I had truly let into my heart. Only one thing would make me do that: I had discovered an untapped pool of bravery. I know that it won't be easy but I want to be with you. I love you! It might be an unconventional love, but I love you all the same. We are meant to be together; I can feel it in my bones.

Where we go from here is all up to you. You call the shots. From now on, you are the captain of my heart.

Love

Eric

Dear Eric

My head is still in a spin. Soon after I got your letter I answered the front door and there you stood. I can honestly say that the lovemaking was the best I've ever had the pleasure of experiencing. In future, you can have your naughty fun with guys if you need to, but don't you dare even look at another woman, mister. I would be green with envy to think that she might be as deeply transported into ecstasy as I am when I am with you.

If I truly call the shots, and I am the captain of your heart, then I say let's go for it. I want to be with you. I want...oh, I want everything: holding hands, romantic picnics, hugs and kisses, lazy mornings in bed. I don't want to scare you off, but I'd love to live with you. Would that be too much to ask?

Love

Marti

Dear Marti

I now know that this is right. I didn't have to think twice about your question. I want to live with you too. The future will take care of itself. I can promise that you will be the only woman for me. I'm coming to get you!

Love

Eric

***

Love Letters from a Lonely Man

Dear Wolf

Ok - let me set out my stall right at the start. It seems really weird to be calling you dear - but that's the way that letters begin, or so I was taught at school - or to be calling a fellow human being Wolf. What ever happened to names like Robert, or James or John? Just so you know, an email address is wasted on me; I don't get the internet here.

I honestly didn't think that I would be writing to you, not after we got the mix up sorted out. I mean, how was I to know that you were a man? The way you looked, and the way you were dressed? I thought the most glamorous woman on earth had descended into our little town. Well, I say our little town, as if I live there, but I think you know what I mean. Perhaps it is the fact that I am so darn lonely on the farm, now that Shandy has left me, that makes me want to write to you.

I still don't understand why you would want to dress the way you did. I mean, where the hell did you put the thing? Forgive my ignorance; I'm just a country hick with no experience of such matters. I didn't realize, at the time, that you were with that big gorilla. It was only after you dashed my hopes on the rocks, with your deep voice and your delight in telling me that you were probably bigger than I was -which I don't doubt; I've always been insecure in that direction - that I saw him put a protective arm around you. By that time you had already given me your business card.

'You're very cute.' you said.

I gulped and blushed. No one had ever said that to me before, least of all another man, and certainly not another man in a dress. I looked at you carefully then, willing it all to be some kind of a hoax. Perhaps you would reveal that you were simply a woman who smoked sixty a day. I couldn't see the slightest sign of stubble, nor an Adam's apple. All I saw were cheekbones that Shandy would have given her makeup kit for and the most stunning babe on the planet. Telling me that I was cute! But also telling me that she had more swinging than I could ever hope for. I felt ill with confusion.

I felt safe back on the farm. I could shut you out of my mind. It had all been a huge mistake and there was no point dwelling on it. Except I couldn't forget you. I couldn't forget those smoky green eyes or those plump, red lips. Couldn't even forget your husky voice, and the things you said. I looked at myself in the mirror and I certainly did not see cute. I saw a forty eight year old man with lines on his face and a receding hairline. I saw tired eyes and a craggy jaw. I saw love handles and a burgeoning butt. Where's the cute in that?

Oh hell! What am I doing writing to you? You are about a million miles away from my life on the farm. What would you know of rising at dawn and working your fingers to the bone? What would you know of coming home to an empty house, or of making love only to my hand, or a bottle of wine? What would I know of your lifestyle? Of dressing up and visiting small town hotel bars. Why? Of hanging out with that dangerous looking man you were with?

I went in to town today and I saw this guy looking at me. I'd heard that he was...you know, like you. Into men. A part of me wanted to be nasty and ask him what he thought he was looking at but another part of me was flattered. I did something out of character; I cupped my hand around my jewels, as though I was having a scratch, except he knew it wasn't a scratch. You should have seen his face! His eyes were about out on stalks then. I panicked and fled, not really sure why I had done what I did. All I knew was I would not know how to handle it if he took that as a sign that I was available.

Because I'm not. I don't want you to go getting any ideas, just because I wrote you a letter. Yes, I'm lonely but that doesn't mean there isn't any elastic in my underpants.

I saw a bird today that I haven't seen around here before. I must look it up in my bird identification guide. I bet that turns you right off, doesn't it. I bet you must think me a real geek, but I don't care. I love nature, and living on a farm. I love being close to nature and understand her rhythms. I bet you like glamour, bright lights, fashion and fine dining.

Why did you give me your card? More to the point is why didn't I just throw it away. Or burn it? Or something...Wolf, I feel like a little piggy living in a straw hut. Is this what you do? Put the moves on vulnerable men, men so lonely that they don't know how to say no to your batting eyelids? I'm beginning to think that you really are a wolf in sheep's clothing.

Can't you uncute me? Tell me that you were drunk and didn't mean it. Tell me that you've bedded a hundred men since you said that. Tell me that you don't even remember my name?

Yours

Martin

Dear Martin

I didn't, even for one minute, think that I would hear from you. I have bedded three men since we met but no, I wasn't drunk and I certainly can not uncute you. The 'gorilla' is just a friend. He looks out for me.

What was I doing in your small town? It's a long, long story but once a sad and confused young man left that little town and headed for the city. I drag up for fun. I had been in town to hear the reading of my late parents' will. I was going to head back home but felt a little emotional and decided to stay. And that's when I decided to dress. I already had all the stuff I needed because I was due to give a show that night in a larger town not too far away. I wondered if anyone would recognize me if I walked into that bar in full regalia. As it turns out, no one did.

I make good money by dressing up and lip synching. The funny thing is I am no longer the person I once thought I was. Years ago I thought the lady in the dress was me, not in a physical way but that she was part of my defence. Now I realize that is no longer true. I do this for fun, and because I'm good at it and because I make a damned good living out of it. I don't wake up in the morning and think 'shit, I have to go in to the office'. No, I lie abed and read and daydream. I take my time having breakfast, and then I do all the chores that need doing. I visit friends, and shop and people watch. And then, in the evening, I have fun putting all the paraphernalia on and then I go out there and knock their sock off.

I've seen love-struck men like you before but in that little town, my home town, I wasn't taking any chances on fouling the nest. You see, I have inherited my parents' house and business. And, strange as it may seem, I think I am beginning to tire of city life and dragging up. I was maybe thinking of coming on home and the last thing I would need is some man hating me for tricking him. That's why I shattered your dream before it even had a chance to turn wet. Sorry.

So, you see, I was surprised to get your letter. Surprised, but pleased. And no, I don't think you are a geek for having a bird identification book. I have one too. There's this couple I know that are big into birding and we go to a nature reserve sometimes on weekends. Perhaps we don't know each other anywhere as much as we think we might. My name is Wilfred and I absolutely hate it. Who on earth calls their kid Wilfred? I'm Wolf now...maybe a big, bad wolf prowling around your door. All those things you told me you saw in the mirror...I love them, especially the beefy butt! I don't think I have ever seen one quite as shapely as yours.

I somehow have a feeling that you won't reply to this letter so I am not going to hold back. I do think you awfully cute and if you were into guys I would be into becoming a farmer's wife. How difficult could it be? All I would have to do is cook and clean, and feed you and look after you and love you. It sounds like my dream job. Oh shit! There I go daydreaming again. I'm prone to that.

So, big farmer dude, the ball is in your court. You could burn this letter and never write again. Or you could write back and give me false hope. If I come back to Unity I could do with a friend, even the most unlikely of friends. Perhaps I could dress for you occasionally and let you daydream too.

Here's something strange. The day I met you I went into the store which I now own and I was looking at the underpants on sale. Call me perverted but I was wondering about the kind of man who would ease his beefy frame into a thirty eight inch pair of undies and now I know. A god on two legs! How can you feel excitement over a scrap of cloth? It made me wonder if there were any other men like me here on the plains. Could I have been the only one, back then? How different my life would have been had I met a man like me all those years ago.

I'm never going to pretend that I don't find you attractive because I do. I find you attractive in a way that I have found no other man attractive. It isn't just sheer physicality; there's a certain something in those sad blue eyes that gets to me. Every time I think about your eyes I find myself fantasizing over and over again and wishing that I could apply for the job of farmer's wife.

Yours

Wolf

Dear Wolf

Where do I start? My head was in a spin, and if I'm honest some other part of me was affected too. I don't know why. In my mind's eye I saw you in that dress and before I knew it things were stirring. I need to find a date. I need to meet a woman who can save me from the wolf at my door. I don't know what the hell is happening to me.

Yours

Martin

Dear Wolf

I thought you might have written back by now. Just because I said the things I did didn't mean you had to back off. I'm the one who is standing too close to the fire. I am the one who should back away.

Something happened today that really upset me. I was in town and I went and bought a couple of pairs of underpants. I suppose I just wanted to be reminded of you. As I left the store I saw my ex-wife walking hand in hand with her new boyfriend. I'd heard that she had a boyfriend so I'm not sure why it was such a shock seeing him, but it was. She introduced me to him and I could feel the ice in my veins. She told me that she was showing him where she had grown up and I wondered if she had a kind word to say about me.

Wolf, I longed for you then. I don't mind admitting it. You are the only one who seems to even know that I exist, let alone have any interest in me. I could see the love shining out of her eyes and I was as jealous as hell. If you had walked by at that moment I think I might have kissed you.

I'm falling deeper and deeper down this well, aren't I? There seems to be no bottom and it has slippery sides. I know the guy running your store; he seems to be doing a good job. Do you really think you would be happy here? What could a little town like this offer a beautiful, exotic butterfly? I'm wearing a pair of those undies as I write. How pathetic is that. What I want is a woman, one that will look after me just the way you want to. Why could you not have been a woman? And yes...I know that's not the whole truth. I want a woman who looks just the way you did that night. I want a woman who will look at me the way you did and tell me that I'm cute. Yes, I know I'm clutching at straws. You must have the worst taste in the world!

Yours

Martin

Dear Martin

You really are some kind of fool, aren't you? I was giving you an out; I was letting you escape. Clearly, you don't want to.

The things you told me in your letter...about buying those undies and wearing them while you wrote to me; you are as weird as I am! And about how you would have given me a kiss if I had walked by while your ex-wife was introducing you to her new boyfriend! And about how you want someone to take care of you. You know that I am ready, willing and able. I don't need money; Rob takes good care of the store. All I need is a roof over my head and someone to love.

Martin, we should quit while we're ahead. So far this has just been a bit of crazy daydreaming. But if we carry on writing to each other someone is going to get hurt, and that someone is me. I can't explain it but you appeal to me in an instinctive way. I can still see your face, whenever I shut my eyes. And I can see the confusion in your eyes when I told you who I really was. We should leave it there. You might meet a woman. I might meet a man.

Yours

Wolf

Dear Wolf

I could never blame you. You offered me an out and I didn't take it. I know not why. I still dream about meeting a woman, a real woman, that I could settle down with and yet I know something has happened to me. I've moved so far from white bread country that I'm practically grinding whole-wheat flour now.

I don't mind telling you that I've had inappropriate thoughts. I have found myself wondering if it really would be so repugnant to...you know. I've gone my whole life without thinking thoughts like that. I didn't even mess around with another guy when I was a horny buck in my early twenties, probably because there wasn't anyone to mess around with. I know that you are dangerous and yet I find you so easy to talk to. A huge part of that must be because I am so lonely but another part must be down to what they call chemistry. And yet, how can we have chemistry when I only met you for such a short time.

Will you be coming back to check on your store at any time? Perhaps we could meet up for a coffee. Even though you seem like this roaring fire that will roast me from a thousand paces I still feel like I want to see you again. I want to see what you look like in your guy clothes. Does that make any sense? If you want to drop by the farm please feel free to do so. It is just eight miles west of Unity and has the unimaginative name of Ranch Q. Not q for queen, but for quest. That was Shandy's idea. I should change it. Perhaps I'll call it Wolf's Den!

Yours

Martin

Dear Wolf

I don't mind telling you that my heart skipped a beat when I saw this vehicle pull up in the yard. I had just had my late breakfast - yes, I have two. I have coffee and a muffin before I go out at first light and then a proper breakfast later - and was about to head back to work. And then I saw this stranger get out of the vehicle and I wasn't sure...I wasn't sure. He looked a little too masculine to be who I thought it might be.

'Martin, it's me.' you said.

I recognized the voice instantly.

'Well look at you, all manned up!' I said.

You laughed and I knew in that moment that I could never feel anything other that positively towards you. No matter where this crazy thing was going I could never hate you, never blame you for what I felt. I'm glad that you called by the farm because I sure as hell would not have recognized you had I had to meet you in a coffee shop.

You asked me for a kiss and I know that you were only being playful but I almost gave in. One of these days I'm going to have to grab this thing by the horns, because a straight man is not supposed to feel the stuff I feel. This whole thing came out of nowhere and has just intensified to the point where all I do is think about you.

Have you thought any further about what you are going to do with the house in Unity? It might be hard to find anyone who wants to rent a house in the back of beyond. A part of me wants you there but another part of me hopes that the city will never let you go. I might be safe then.

Yours

Wolf

Dear Martin

Your heart is not the only one that skipped a beat. I had forgotten how beautiful you are. When I asked for a kiss I was only half joking. When I saw you pretend you lean in I thought I was about to have a full-blown heart attack.

I think the city is starting to lose its grip on me. I've not worked for weeks now, though I keep getting calls from anxious club owners. I just can't deal with it any more. Miss Kitty has left the building, I fear. I see this big house on the edge of town, with a large garden and plenty of bird life. And that's where I see my future more and more. I've asked Rob to get someone to carry on some decorating work that I want done.

Don't let what I want panic you. There's no need to see me, or even to be friends, if you don't want to. I know that you need a woman. You know that I am a man. I'm never going to dress again. That's where things stand. I'd love for us to be friends, obviously. No, I'm lying; I'd love for us to be more than friends. I'd love to be the one to wave you off to work each morning. I'd get up at the crack of dawn for a man like you. Oh fuck! This is never going to work, is it? We're just being stupid.

Yours

Wolf

Dear Wolf

There's something I need to tell you. I owe you that much. Some friends in town have lined up a mystery date for me. Of course I said yes. I couldn't say no after going on about how I would love a date. And how could I tell them that there were added complications. I don't understand this little man-crush so I don't expect that they will.

I went into your store to get some new clothes. And yes, I bought some more undies. Rob must think I have some sort of fetish. How come you don't fancy him? He is a big guy too. I think if I was into guys I would go for Rob; there's just so much of him to hold onto.

See, this is how sick I am...I am writing to you to tell you that I am going on a date with a woman and yet I am telling you about buying underpants, which I know will turn you on. I bought some purple ones and some red ones; they seem rather racy!

I wish that I could return to normal and perhaps I will after this date. Perhaps we will hit it off and date some more and who knows what might happen then? My dear Wolf, I hope you meet the man of your dreams. No, not the coward you met but one who wants you as much as you want him.

Take care

Martin

Dear Martin

I'm happy for you, really I am. You deserve to be happy and I know that only a woman can make you happy. We came close but eight inches are always going to get in the way, aren't they?

Rob is a lovely man, and there is plenty of him to hold onto, but he is not my kind. Besides, he is my employee! I need him to run the store while I'm still getting my act together and trying to decide if I really could give up city life. Perhaps I'm just going through a phase, brought on by meeting a certain gorgeous farmer.

I went home with a man for the first time in ages last night. I was watching my replacement act - she really is not too bad - and I got chatting to this guy at the bar. He could tell that I was sad and that I was pining for someone. It turns out that he is a farmer too. Well, as soon as I heard that I stood no chance of resisting him. He is a lovely, sweet man, and he makes love like a dream, but sadly he is married and I'm done with that.

Good luck with your date. May she be the woman of your dreams.

Yours

Wolf

Dear Wolf

Why am I so fucking jealous? I keep thinking about you and that man in bed together. The fact that he is married just makes it worse. I apparently am not the only straight man who has had his head turned by you.

Dream date? More like the date from hell. Mandy is desperate to be a farmer's wife, even more so than you are. She left me no wriggle room. In the end I told her that I was struggling with my sexuality and felt that maybe now was not the right time to be dating. Well, that went down like a lead balloon. Stan came to see me and demanded to know what was going on. I was going to tell him the truth; tell him that I had felt hemmed in by Mandy's neediness, but then I realized the truth was that I had feelings for a certain guy. So I told him the truth, the whole truth and nothing but the truth. You should have seen his face! It was as if I had asked him to take off his pants and bend over the sofa.

I guess my dating days are at an end. I should imagine my name is mud in Unity at the moment. How can I explain to anyone that, although I am a straight man, I have feelings for a gay guy? It's far too complicated. I know that I wouldn't have believed such a thing just a few short months ago.

What am I going to do about you?

Yours

Martin

Dear Martin

I drove past Ranch Q today. I was tempted to call in but decided it best not to. I can't tell you what to do about me, other than give me a beef injection. I can't even advise you. Only you know what you need to do.

Rob has been his usual efficient self and the decorations have been completed. The house now looks like I want it to and I have decided that I am going to move in. I've promised Rob that I won't interfere with the running of the business; just so long as the profits keep rolling in I'll be happy. I see he has restocked on thirty eighty inch waist underpants. When I asked him about it he said some big guy keeps buying up his stock. He told me that this mystery buyer would be right up my street. I had to smile. If only he knew. If only all men were as gay friendly as Rob is.

I had no idea just how gay friendly Rob is. I suggested that we go out to lunch, to celebrate the complete of the redecoration, and there was this guy waiting our table that Rob seemed to know very well. He told me that Lane was a good customer and we got chatting and I could tell that Lane was into guys.

'I bet he would be happy if you came back to Unity.' Rob said.

'Do you think?'

'Did you not see the way he looked at you?' Rob asked. 'He used to look at me like that once.'

'Didn't you mind?' I asked.

'My wife doesn't like it.' Rob said. 'It doesn't bother me that much. It's nice to know that someone still finds me attractive. I think Lisa only sees safe, dependable Rob these days.'

I wiped away a tear then, partly because of what Rob had just told me and partly because I was thinking of someone else.

'Don't ever believe that you're not attractive.' I told Rob.

'I guess I'm just a little insecure.' Rob said. 'You've never looked at me like Lane did.'

'You are my employee!' I pointed out. 'Besides, it's not that I don't think you are attractive; there's a guy I've met and...well, things are complicated.'

'You're going to leave him behind in the city?' Rob asked.

'Not quite. It's really complicated.' I said. 'It feels like something is calling me back to Unity. I guess things will get resolved one way or another.'

'I hope that Lane gets lucky.' Rob said. 'He is awfully lonely here in Unity but he doesn't have the courage to leave.'

So, big man, as I said before, the ball is in your court. Only you know what you need and want. What I want is you. There, I've said it. I want nothing less, and nothing more. And, I guess if you don't want me then maybe Lane will get lucky.

Yours

Wolf

Dear Wolf

No! Absolutely not. Lane needs to get to the back of the queue. I might not know exactly what I want but I have a fairly good idea. I do not want any other man kissing up on you. Please could you give me a little time to sort my head out? Don't rush into anything, huh? It sounds to me like that Rob is almost as dangerous as Lane is. Who knew that Unity is seething with manlust?

Yours

Martin

Dear Martin

It seems strange to be writing to you from Unity. Yep! I cut my ties with the city and moved in. Rob and Lisa were really kind and helped me enormously. I am now a gentleman of leisure. I've signed up for a creative wring course and I am planning on writing steamy erotica about lonely farmers with love handles and sturdy thighs.

I had a chat with Lane today and I explained how things are with me right now. He agreed to wait a couple of months to see what develops before he puts the moves on me. I have no doubt that I shall not be able top resist once he starts his seduction routine. He has the longest lashes I have ever seen on a guy and when he looks at you it's like he is looking right into you soul!

Yours

Wolf

Dear Martin

I could not believe it when I answered the doorbell last night and there you were. You looked even more gorgeous than I remembered and those rugby shorts you were wearing were positively criminal. I've always wondered if your legs are as hairy as you arms and now I know.

I thought at first you had come to tell me that you had made up your mind that you couldn't see me. And then you picked me up and carried me into the bedroom and made love to me in the sweetest way! I was over the moon and kept thinking that I would soon wake from this crazy dream.

You insisted that we go out to eat and, to be safe, I took you to the only other restaurant in town that did not employ a waiter named Lane. How was I to know that Lane would be in there? Although, to be fair, he looked rather guilty as he had a very hot number him. Oh, how you gloated when I pointed Lane out. You placed your large hand on mine and looked directly at him I think he got the message. I was sad for Lane but too far gone on love to care.

When you told me to order the finest bottle of wine in the house I asked if you were not worried about having to drive later. That's when you told me that you were planning on leaving at 5 AM. My joy knew no bounds. A whole night with you! A night filled with kisses, caresses and dirty-hot sex!

But now, here I am down in the dumps again. I need more. I need to know that you might come visit me again. Or was this just you getting the guy thing out of your system? After all, every straight man is allowed to mess up once, right?

Do I have to grovel and beg you for more of your sweet love? Or do I have to beg Lane for forgiveness?

Love

Wolf

Dear Wolf

If it seems strange that you should write to me from Unity it seems even stranger for me to be collecting your letters in Unity.

I won't lie. I have been conflicted. The sex was incredible; I had no idea. But you're a guy and I'm a guy. Whose ideas get to take precedence? I know that you are strong-willed and much more liberal than I am. Won't you get bored of this son of the earth? I'm nowhere near as sophisticated as you are. I don't read or think about things too deeply. I know you said you want to take care of me but isn't that just a fantasy. Won't you tire of domestic bliss after a week and long for Lane's long lashes, or Rob's gay-friendly ways?

Love

Martin

Dear Martin

It is time you get a grip. It is only sheer willpower that keeps me from driving out to Ranch Q and nailing that beefy butt of yours.

Do you not think I've thought about all the things you asked me about? I've done nothing but think about them and the answer is always that I want to be with you. Lane is nice, but he is not you. Rob might have a weak spot but I'm not going to be the one to exploit it. My life is complicated enough with one straight man in it, thank you very much.

Martin, I want to wake up with you. If it was practical I would ask you to move in with me. If you don't want to go that far then how about letting me visit two or three nights a week.

Love

Wolf

Dear Wolf

I should have known that I could trust you to come up with the solution. I'm scared, I don't mind admitting that, but I don't want to back away now. I've come on a long journey but there's still a long way to go.

I saw Stan recently and told him that I had made love with a man. He said he didn't understand it but that he would learn to get used to the idea, given time. That's when I told him how unused to the idea I was. He laughed and we went and had a beer then, and we chatted things through. He told me that it wasn't too late to change my mind but I realize that it is. I am in love with a man. There aint nothing I can do to change that. It's strange, I felt so distant from Stan and yet also felt I had never been closer to him.

How about you come through to the farm twice a week and I will come to Unity once a week? I know that you are a hungry pup but you have to remember that I am ten years older than you!

Love

Martin

Dear Martin

I sure hope that you pick up this letter by Friday because I'm coming to claim my prize on Friday. I've not felt this optimistic about the future for a very long time! I'll calm down, given time, and perhaps won't want you as desperately as I do now. But, for now, every time I look at you I just want to make love to you. I can't help it!

Love always

Wolf

***

Love Letters from Space

Dear Maura

Looking out of the window, at the little blue marble, reminds me how far away from you I am. It's so lonely here in outer space. Yes, I have scientists and technicians around me but they have not yet learned the ways of the heart. They are cold, efficient...ruthless even, and sometimes I find it hard to believe that these are my people.

I am telling you this now because we have drawn closer to each other and I can tell that you are troubled by my reticence to talk about certain things. Pray that I were an ordinary man, doing an ordinary job! How simple things would be. If you have not already guessed it, I am not one of your race. I am what you call an alien. If I had any sense I would have walked away before it became necessary to share this secret with you.

I miss your laughter, which is like the tinkling of keys on a piano or a bubbling brook. I miss the inner-fire in your eyes; they are always so alive, so inquisitive and convey so much with just one look. All these things are new to me: music, art and a sense of humor. All we know is war, survival and empire building. We have no need to laugh, no need to cry. We have no need to feel, or think; our lives are mapped out from the day we are created in a sterile laboratory. What we need to know about is how to travel through space, how to guarantee the resources we need and how to subdue. If I say it myself, we are excellent at these things.

It amuses me to think that your people think that humans are alone in this world. You should see all the peoples I've seen. If you can call them that! Some you would not even recognize as life forms. I'm talking three heads, no heads, heads on knees, etc. Some are placid and are easily vanquished. Others fight tooth and claw until we have to move on, with a promise to return another day. The machine demands that we always conquer, always vanquish and that we take the raw materials that we need to protect our empire. I'm so tired of this existence, especially now that you have shown me another way.

How simple are your pleasures there on earth. When you took me to that waterfall I was in awe of how in awe of the waterfall you were. Perhaps I have seen too much. On planet Veskon there are waterfalls a hundred times the size of the one we saw that day. There are mountains fifty times taller than Everest. Perhaps you will forgive me if I seem disinterested; I am not, but I don't have any easy way of showing it. Emotions don't come easily to me. If something is not programmed into me at the point of creation it takes a while for me to get to grips with it, especially if it is not a science that I can study, and measure.

You do know that I am no good for you, don't you? I am so very far from what you need. I have to learn the nuance of each emotion, each glance and each touch of the hand. The things which you humans take for granted are like a broken computer screen to me. Here is something you might difficult to comprehend: while we are apart I live through a month in your time, aging a little more, and getting closer to the time when I need to be rebooted. Soon I will have to go for regeneration and that will wipe clean the memory of my mind. The idea of losing you in this way is unbearable. Yes, I will have the body I need to keep travelling through space, to keep waging war and securing the ores we need but I won't have you. I feel so alone. There is not a single one of my people who understands the concept of love, who understands what you mean to me. I am totally alone in this.

Yet, for all this, I cannot stop thinking about you. I will not let go of you until you let go of me. I love the sound of your voice and the sound of your laughter, in as much as I can love. I don't know how long my rebellious streak will be tolerated; I don't know if the council will call me in and tell me that my brain is to be reconfigured to wipe away the emotions I have learned. The council knows everything: they must know the turmoil in my mind.

Why would you want someone like me? What good could I ever be to you? My life is not my own. I am but a cog in the machine. I was created to serve the Uber Empire. I was taught the science I need to travel across time and space, collecting data and searching for valuable minerals. Back on Jyrkad resources are in short supply. We have the greatest minds in the universe but no minerals, no ores; we are forced to travel and conquer. Only Earth has proved beyond our power to subdue. Your governments keep hidden from their people how often they have to neutralize threats from outer space. To the best of my knowledge only Jyrkadians have been able to breach earth's defences and that is probably because we are such good chameleons. Our craft look as innocuous as your airplanes and you have already seen how indistinguishable I am from a human.

We observe, with greed and envy, all of Earth's resources and technology. Some Jyrkadians, such as I, are given earthly form so that we might travel amongst your peoples, looking for a weakness, some easy way in. You are probably committing treason by not reporting me to the authorities. Yet what good would it do. Should they capture me I would simply change form and escape. Should they remove me from earth a replacement will be there within the hour.

I have never told you all these things before because I did not want to alarm you. All I said was that I was different. Now that you know how different I am, I leave it up to you to do whatever it is your head and heart tells you to do. Report me to the authorities, tell me you don't want to see me anymore; do whatever feels right for you.

Whatever you decide I shall always have a tender place in my under-used heart for you.

Flordis

Dear Flordis

Your memory fails you; you did once tell me that you were a spaceman when I asked about your work. I thought perhaps the space stuff was something you said just to make yourself seem more interesting. I see now that you were not joking. I should have challenged you, as I thought it mildly eccentric, but why waste the precious time we have together. So, my boyfriend is slightly odd, I thought, but what of it. He is tender and kind, he values me as a person and he isn't in a headlong rush to get my panties off.

It is too late for me...I have fallen in love with you and I don't care about anything else. Even if you told me that you had three heads (most of the time) I wouldn't care. I'm in too deep. I'm impressed to know that that you have had to learn about emotions from scratch. You have always seemed so sensitive, so in tune with my needs that I find it really difficult to believe that this does not come naturally to you.

I'll admit that some of the things you told me are worrying. I don't like the idea of you aging a month while I age just a day. But worse than that, is the regeneration thing. They can wipe your memory? It scares me to think that they can erase all we have had together in just a flash. It seems cruel that they can take away something so beautiful.

Flordis, I love you with all of my heart. You are kind and strong and you never make a fuss. Nothing is too much trouble for you. Sometimes it feels as though you can read my mind. Hah! You probably can. I sure hope that you can't though. I'd be embarrassed if you knew the lusty thoughts that swirl around inside my brain.

I'm thinking about you, wherever you are, and can't wait until I see you again.

Love

Maura

Dear Maura

No, I cannot read your mind. Our people might be clever but we are not that clever. I don't think I understand what lust is. No doubt you will explain it to me when next we meet.

I have just collected some core samples from a planet named Drigbran. You should see the people there: they stand no more than a foot high and have beards down to their little feet. Every single one of them has a long, grey beard! How they shook their little fists at our space craft. I felt sorry for them. This is perhaps why my people do not have emotions. We are always snatching, grabbing and stealing. Being emotional makes this job so much more difficult. Yet without emotions I could not enjoy your company and I would not change that.

Promise me that if you are ever wiped from my memory, you will attempt to find me again. I sometimes think that you must have extra sensory powers. I always feel so calm when I am with you. I feel as though none of the awful things I have done and seen, in service of the empire, matter anymore. Your love and understanding wipe the slate clean. There are times when I wish that I was a mere mortal. We could be so happy together.

I will be back on earth soon, in your timescale, that is. I look forward to seeing your lovely smile again. The memory of you keeps me company as I fly around in such lonely places as you could not imagine. I should think that brilliant smile of yours could light up any darkness. Sometimes it feels so lonely flying through the inky blackness. I could do with your radiance at times like these.

Missing you

Flordis

Dear Flordis

It was so wonderful to see you again! How I wished you could have stayed longer and that I could have discussed with you all that was in my heart.

Are you afraid of me? Is that why you always want to meet me in public spaces? Are you afraid I might jump your bones?

I'm sitting on the sofa with a bottle of wine and a weepy movie for company. How pathetic is that? 'You should get out more...find a boyfriend' my friends tell me. If only they knew I already have the most wonderful boyfriend in the world. Of course they would never believe the space thing; I think they would probably tell me to go see a psychiatrist. Sometimes, I can't believe the space thing either. What are the chances of me falling in love with an alien!

Alien, or not, I can't wait until I see you again. I wish that you were able to visit me every day but I understand that your duties prevent this. At least I hope it is your duties, and not a case that you have women all over this planet.

Love

Maura

Dear Maura

I don't feel very good at the moment. I know that on the outside I look like any healthy thirty year old man but inside I'm aging fast. All this space travel is taking its toll. Soon I will have to submit to regeneration. Believe me, I have neither the energy nor the desire to have anyone else but you.

I hate the fact that you are lonely without me and that I am making you miserable. Your friends are right: you should find a boyfriend. What about that guy you chatted to when we were strolling through the park. He looks fit and healthy and I think he is keen on you.

I hate it when you feel sad. I hate even more that it is me making you feel sad. If you had never met me you would not have wasted your emotions on me. I'm sure there must be loads of sensitive guys down there on earth. You just have to find the right one.

So sad

Flordis

Dear Flordis

Not another word about boyfriends! There can only ever be one man for me.

What would happen were you not to return to space? Could you not just stay here with me? Nothing would make me happier. To have you as my lover, constantly by my side, would make me the happiest woman on earth. I'm so ready to surrender to pleasure and passion. Please do not be afraid; we have known each other long enough. I cannot imagine anything more pleasurable than surrendering to you. I am an old fashioned girl and I have never enjoyed the physical side of relationships before. I realize now that there was not enough love and respect for me to feel comfortable with the experience. All of that has changed now. I'm ready to blossom.

I don't like what your job is doing to you, and I don't enjoy knowing that the conflict you feel is all my fault. If I hadn't taught you to love, and to feel, you would feel no regret about the work you do. I certainly couldn't do it. How I feel for those little bearded people who are about to have their planet destroyed, all for the sake of a few minerals. However, I don't think I would like to have a long, grey beard! I wonder how the women on that planet cope. On the other hand, having a beard means they never have to worry about shaving their legs.

Love

Maura

Dear Maura

If I were not to return to space I would simply be recalled. One minute I would be there and the next I would be gone. I'm surprised that the authorities haven't figured out how much time I am spending with you. They probably just think that I am being a really good spy.

Not all planets have different sexes. On some planets people (if you can call of them that) multiply simply by dividing in two and forming a replica copy of themselves. Did you see what I did there...multiply by dividing. Is that what you call humor? I hope that I am learning. I'd love to make you laugh more. You are so sweet when you laugh.

It is only on planet earth that females are so occupied with looks. If you lived on a planet on which all the women had long, grey beards I shouldn't think it would matter what you looked like. And the men would love women with long grey beards. I would still love you if you had fifteen eyes and a dozen noses although I do prefer the way you look now.

I wish you were here in the spaceship with me. I would have some real company then. My companions on the ship know nothing of companionship, or humor or fun. All they know is how to collect, collate and analyze. Sometimes, I'll forget where I am and make a little joke and they will look at me askance, as if I'm from another planet. Anyway, it wouldn't be fair to bring you on board. By the end of one of our months you would have aged three years, provided that you survived being up here in the first place.

I realize that I am being unfair. There is no hope for us, is there? I should let you go and leave you free to love someone who is right for you. I should insist that you do this but I'm weak.

Love

Flordis

Dear Flordis

Please don't say such things. You are right for me. You make my heart sing. I would follow you to the ends of the world if I had to, though I suspect I might not survive the lift off into space. We humans have to spend a long time preparing to travel beyond our world and the places you go to are still beyond our science.

You are developing quite a sense of humor. I love it! It is just one more thing to love about you. You are so perfect in every way. My only regret is that you are such a gentleman. We have known each other long enough now, don't you think? Sometimes I just wish you would ravish me. There, I've said it. I have needs which are going unfulfilled.

Love

Maura

Dear Maura

What is this 'ravish'? I don't understand. This reminds me that there is so much which I still need to learn.

You would have loved the planet I landed on yesterday. There were about fifteen different sexes, all subtly different from each other. Talk about exhibitionists! They couldn't wait to show me all their bits. Which brings me on to something that I have to tell you.

I have been avoiding this situation for as long as I can. The reason I have been 'such a perfect gentleman' is that I have no way of making love to you. I have no genitals. They are not needed on our planet as each one of us is created in a laboratory. I've seen how your eyes glaze over when people kiss in the movies you watch. I've researched this and seen who does what to whom. I had hoped that our silly little crush would have long run its course before we got to this point. I had hoped that you would have grown tired of me and moved on to a real man, one who has the necessary equipment.

I feel so embarrassed telling you this. I should have told you this a long time ago but I didn't want to lose you. Some of us are given the necessary equipment when it is deemed necessary but I was not one of the lucky ones.

If you want me to stay away please tell me to and I will. Though it would make me sad, I know it is the best thing to do.

Love

Flordis

Dear Flordis

Ravish means make love to, but in an intense way. I am
sorry if I have embarrassed you. You look so much like
an ordinary man I thought you were the same in every
respect. I don't mind if you have no genitals; I still want
you in my bed. You have a pair of hands and two lips,
do you not?

My love, you are the kindest, sweetest man I have ever
met. When I am with you I feel happy and content. Had
I known that you were different from other men I would
not have brought up the subject. Please forgive me. We
will find a way to have a meaningful physical
relationship and I'm big on cuddles. Don't be afraid. I
only want to be with you.

Love

Maura

Dear Maura

What am I going to do with you? I tell you the most
devastating piece of news and you still want me? Do you
know what you are letting yourself in for? There is
nothing down there; just smooth skin. The men on earth
seem to take such pride in their rampant rods that I
thought they were supremely significant. Yes I have
hands and lips and I am sure I can learn what to do but
there are so many obstacles in our way.

The council has given me a date for my regeneration. It
is not far off. Whatever we have together will be
snatched away. How will I even find you again if I can't
remember you? Sometimes I feel like snatching you
away from earth and carrying you off beyond the stars.
Just you and me... flying along through the darkness and
making love whenever you wanted. You know how I
said I didn't believe you would survive the lift off from

earth? I've never told you this before because you would hate me for it but we have abducted earthlings in the past. They all seemed to start ailing as soon as we lifted off into space and none lived beyond six months. I cannot allow such a fate to befall you.

My beautiful Maura, it is time to end this madness. I cannot live on earth and you cannot live in space. Even if we could live together I could never give you a baby and I know how much you would like to be a mother. Be brave, walk away from me and find your perfect man. He is out there somewhere.

Love

Flordis

Dear Flordis

Is that six months in earth time or in Jyrkad time?

Love

Maura

Dear Maura

Six months in Jyrkad time; a month of days lasting a month. Why?

Love

Flordis

Dear Flordis

Six months in Jyrkad time is like forever. That's plenty of time for us to be together. Steal that space craft and let's run away together. Be with me until they find you and snatch you away for regeneration. Teach me how to find you after you have been regenerated, if that is possible. You have learnt much of our ways down here on earth and now I'm ready to learn your ways.

There can never be another man for me. Your love has spoiled me. I am willing to trade my future for six months on the run with you. I have never felt so live before; meeting you was the best thing that ever happened to me. Please, no more chaste walks in the park. I need to be kissed like fifty million times.

Love

Maura

Dear Maura

I felt close to crying when I read your letter. See what you've done to me! Jyrkadians have no need for tears yet I wanted to blub. I cannot let you do what you are proposing. You surely do not mean it when you say you are willing to give up your life for me. This is crazy. Think about all the things you would be missing out on.

Please, be sensible. Stop loving me and find that man you need. You are a beautiful woman, inside and out. You are caring, loving and giving. You will make someone a wonderful wife. You can have the family you long for. You can even have that white picket fence, although I have to say that I don't understand this at all.

I found this little poem and it seems to say everything I am trying to tell you.

Sometimes love
Demands that you walk away
Sometimes you reach the end of the line
Still in love
But there's no other way
Sometimes fate conspires against you
And you cannot entwine
Be brave; walk away
Love will visit again
Another day

I'll understand if you no longer want to see me. Just give me the word and I will leave you in peace.

Love

Flordis

Dear Flordis

The only man I need is you. When are you going to get that into your thick head?

We don't know for certain that I would die after six months. Perhaps all those people died out of loneliness and frustration. Remember, I would have you by my side. I would have all that I want and need. It is time for you to man up and come down and fetch me.

I'm ready to follow you through time and space. I want to see the wonders that you see. I would gladly trade another four or five decades here on earth just to be with you. This love I feel cannot be undone.

Each rose is surrounded by thorns
He who will tame the bull
Must grasp its horns
I will not be weak

I am made of sterner stuff
Let fate wave its cape
I will prepare my charge
And kick up the dust
I'll be defiant and head strong
For in with the smooth
There always has to be some rough
Trust a woman in love
She is never wrong

Love

Maura

Dear Maura

Something major has happened. The council suddenly
called me in for regeneration, ahead of schedule. I
wanted to run away and hide but, of course, resistance is
futile. I had absolutely no say in the matter. As I waited
to enter the laboratory I kept on saying your name to
myself, over and over. I was certain that this was the end
of the line for us. I told myself that if I tried hard enough
to reach you, you would know that you were loved. If I
were to come out of the process with no memory of you,
at least I would have tried to send you a message to let
you know just how much you mean to me. If I've never
said it before, you mean everything to me.

I used to worry that I was simply absorbing your
emotions, not really feeling them for myself. Now I
know that's not true. I have been on a roller coaster ride
of emotion these last few days. Before I forget, I want to
tell you I can now understand how you see the world. I
want to share that with you. I want to grow and feel. I'm
not afraid to be afraid, or vulnerable. And I am certainly
not afraid to love. My beautiful Maura, you have given
me the most precious gift in the universe.

Something happened during the regeneration process; I have forgotten almost everything apart from you. My memory of you is sharper, keener. I shed tears of joy when I realized what had happened. It was almost as if chanting your name had protected me. I found myself wondering if the council knew what had happened to me. As a test I went up to them and said your name. Their eyes glazed over. I don't think they had a clue what I was talking about. Somehow your name has protected our love; your name has evicted the council from the deepest recesses of my brain. We have a safe space, my love.

We now have hope. I have not been reassigned away from duties on earth, which is something I had feared. I will be there tomorrow!

Oh, I almost forgot to tell you! I somehow look five years younger than I did before and I feel in fine form. And, here's the big thing, after the regeneration process I looked down and realized I'd struck gold. Yes, they've only gone and given me all the bits I need. I think there must have been some sort of malfunction during the regeneration process but I'm not going to worry about that. I've got my health, my memory and, you know...that, and I've got you. What more could any man ask for?

Prepare to be ravished!

All my love

Flordis

Can't Help Falling

No! I wasn't happy; not in the least. It was Friday evening and I had been looking forward to a nice, long soak in the tub, and then some time spent on my crossword puzzles and then a wonderful meal, accompanied by some excellent wine, and then perhaps we would watch a movie after that and then go to bed, in separate beds, in separate bedrooms, of course. But now there was some big fellah sitting in my armchair. What was the meaning of this?

'Marty, this is Ben. Ben, Marty.' Adrian said. 'Ben's driving across country and needed somewhere to crash for the night.'

'Oh.' I replied as I shook hands.

Something didn't feel quite right to me. What was wrong with the local hotel? Sure, it wasn't luxurious but it was clean, and decent. Where had this Ben character suddenly sprang from? And would Adrian be creeping into his bed at night? Not that it was any of my business, you understand. I've always known that Adrian likes guys; I guess sooner of later he was bound to bring a guy home. Maybe I'm getting too far ahead of myself. Forgive me if I don't know how to tell a story; I never thought I would want to.

I am the invisible man you never notice. I am short, and stocky, balding, with unremarkable looks and on the wrong side of forty. My ex wife used to say that I have too much booty and not enough legs. She used to want me to get my butt cheeks waxed, but I wasn't having any of that. She also used to say that when God was handing out cocks the wind must have been blowing hard and I didn't hear him. I suppose her new beau is hung like a horse and has buns of steel which are as smooth as alabaster. Despite all the horrible things she used to say to me I still miss her, and would take her back immediately if she were to walk through the front door. Which aint going to happen. Besides, she'd be somewhat confused as to why I'm living with Adrian.

The guys at work have given up on me. They're convinced that I've gone over to the other side. They absolutely cannot understand why I would want to live with a gay guy if I hadn't jumped over the fence to his side of the field. They call him my boyfriend and I just let them get on with it.

'How is your boyfriend?' someone might ask on a Monday morning.

'Fine.' I'll reply.

'Get plenty of action over the weekend, did you?'

'Yeah. Whatever.'

It is so much easier than trying to explain. I'm not sure that I really understand it myself. All I know is that Adrian makes me feel like a king, and I could get addicted to that, if I'm not already. He is a real good cook and an excellent baker; he is calm and kind and understanding and quirky and funny too, into the bargain. Of course I was wary of him at first, but he has never once tried it on with me. I guess my ex-wife was right; I just don't have what it takes to float his boat, but we get along real well. At first I used to just visit on a Friday night. I was bored with going to the one-and-only bar in town, and seeing the same people, and listening to them telling the same boring stories. Hanging out with Adrian seemed a much better alternative.

Adrian was always able to surprise me, and he still can. He has travelled to places I've never even dreamed of going, and is interested in stuff I have never even heard of. What is really wonderful about him, though, is he never makes me feel stupid, or unsophisticated, or small. It didn't take long before I started visiting two or three times a week. It saved me having to cook and he is so much better at it than I am. I was hesitant the first time he asked me if I wanted to sleep over. I said yes, though my head was telling me to say no. I half expected him to come creeping into my room - despite never having shown any physical interest in me - but he did not. So, when he asked me if I wanted to move in a few months later it was a no-brainer. All I had to do was come home in the evening and be treated like royalty. What was not to love about that?

It didn't matter to me what people thought. The news had spread like wildfire when I first slept over. Someone had seen me leaving Adrian's house in the early hours of the morning and by lunch time everyone I knew was convinced that I was about to come out of the closet and sing 'I Will Survive'. Like I told you earlier, I'm pretty invisible anyway, so what did it matter what a few people thought?

But now Ben was sitting in my armchair, and I wasn't sure about the connection between him and Adrian. There was something about the way they looked at each other, like they had history. Darned right, I didn't want to sleep with Adrian, but that didn't mean that I wanted Ben to either. I know, I know...that's weird, huh, but it's how I feel.

'Marty, would you mind letting Ben have your bed tonight?' Adrian asked me.

'Guys, I can sleep on the couch.' Ben said.

'You're far too tall for that.' Adrian pointed out. 'You would not get a comfortable night's sleep.'

'Sure, no problem.' I said.

Suddenly I didn't feel so bad. If Adrian and I shared a bed it meant I could keep an eye on him and, more importantly, I could make sure that Ben wasn't in his bed. I went off and had my bath and then spent a little time chatting to Ben while Adrian fixed a meal. Wow!

He really pulled out all the stops that night. It was food fit for a king.

'You're a lucky man, Marty.' Ben said. 'Adrian is a wonderful cook.'

'Don't I know it!' I replied. 'I think that he is trying to make sure that no woman ever looks at me again by making me put on weight.'

'You're straight?' Ben asked.

'Yes. Why?'

'Sorry, I just assumed.'

Adrian just smiled.

'I guess I shouldn't assume anything, should I?' Ben said.

'Probably not.' I said. 'How about you? Are you gay?'

'Kinda bi, now and then.' Ben said.

'Can't make up your mind?' I asked.

'It's not really that.' he said. 'I'm mostly straight but just occasionally I'll meet a gay guy who turns my head.'

So I was right, I told myself. Adrian and Ben had history, and I was pretty cheesed off about it.

'Were you two...?' I couldn't form the words.

'A long time ago.' Ben said. 'I couldn't give Adrian what he wanted. He wanted a man who would come home to him every evening, not some guy who slipped away from his girlfriend every now and then.'

I squirmed.

'How long have you two been sharing a house?' Ben asked me.

'Seven months now.' I replied.

'I'm so glad that Adrian has someone to take care of; he always needed that.' Ben said.

'We're not, you know...' I said.

'I know.' he replied. 'But you're close; I can tell. '

'The guys at work think I'm having a relationship with Adrian.' I said. 'They just can't understand the dynamic between us.'

'Well, we can't always change what people think so we have to just let them get on with it.' Ben pointed out.

It felt really weird walking into Adrian's bedroom that night and stripping down to my undies and getting into bed. He climbed into bed and said goodnight and I was soon asleep. However, something woke me from sleep and I realized that Adrian was no longer in bed. I knew it! He had snuck away to be with Ben. Why the hell didn't he just have Ben sleep in his bed, I wondered. I was hopping mad, thinking about what I would say to him when he reappeared. And then I heard a flush in the bathroom and he climbed back into bed soon after.

I was so relieved that I slid behind him and took him into my arms.

'I thought you had snuck out to be with Ben.' I said.

'I'm never going back down that road.' Adrian said. 'It hurt too much.'

'I'm sorry.' I replied.

'This is nice.' he said.

'No sex, you understand.' I said. 'If you promise to be good I might just cuddle you all night long.'

'I promise.' he replied.

'Just ignore the little traitor in my undies.' I told him. 'I don't know what he is getting so excited for.'

Adrian just chuckled and placed his hand on mine. It was warm and soft and reassuring, but at the same time I wondered if he would try to move my hand down his body to where he wanted it to be. However, I need not have worried. Adrian was true to his word and we both drifted off to sleep soon after. When I woke in the morning he was still in my arms and my cock was still throbbing. I don't mind telling you that I had to whack one out while I was in the shower. Talk about a guilt trip.

Adrian fixed breakfast and we sat outside on the patio, listening to birdsong and thinking our private thoughts. I wondered if Ben wondered if we had made love. What would he have thought of me if he knew that I had cuddled Adrian all night long? And what would Ben, and Adrian, have thought about the fact that I had jerked off in the shower that morning while trying to fight off the memory of Adrian's peachy little ass snuggled up close to my throbbing prick?

Ben had to hit the road soon after breakfast and it was just me and Adrian alone again, just like it always was on a Saturday morning.

'What are you going to do today?' I asked.

'I er...I think I might head on up to the city.'

'What?' I was shocked. 'Just like that? It's a long way to go.'

'I need something...something I can't get here.' his voice was barely above a whisper.

'What? Cock?' I spat.

He nodded.

'Please don't go.' I said.

'What is it to you?' he asked.

'You don't know...' I could not continue.

'I don't know what?' he asked.

'Look, there's stuff going on.' I said. 'I just can't say at the moment.'

'You don't want me to get laid?'

'No.' I said.

'Well, at least you're honest.' he replied. 'If I don't go this weekend, I'll have to go the next. I can't carry on like this.'

'It's Ben; he has unsettled you.' I said.

'How do you figure that?' he sounded angry.

'What are you so cross about?' I asked.

'The man I love holds me close all night long and I am fucking horny. Is it too much for me to want to get this out of my system?'

'I know that I'm being unreasonable but please don't leave me alone this weekend.' I said. 'I'll come and sleep in your bed again if you promise to stay.'

His face softened. He managed a half smile.

'You promise?'

'Absolutely.'

I kept myself busy with chores all day because there was stuff I didn't want to think about. Deep down inside I knew I was never again going to get together with a woman. I was stuck in a dead end job in a little town in the back of beyond and I didn't even own a vehicle. What prospects did I have? I could never sweep anyone off their feet when I hardly had two cents to rub together. I also knew, deep down and though I didn't want to admit it to myself, that I would always want to live with Adrian. I had learned to get by on a couple of wank sessions a month; why couldn't he? Why couldn't the two of us carry on the way we had been until we drew our last breath? I was happy, secure and comfortable and that was more than I could say for my last few years with Hailey.

Adrian had been up to the city once before and left me alone at home at the weekend. I had fretted, wondering if he was safe. I had visions of him approaching strangers in some seedy alleyway and getting the shit kicked out of him. How could he just have sex with a stranger? Sure, I had fantasized about it but I knew that I would never be able to make that fantasy a reality. As if anyone would want to be with me, anyway. And yet...hadn't Adrian said 'last night the man that I love held me in his arms'? This was the first time that I knew how he felt. I had always just assumed that we were just good buddies, that I didn't do anything for him. Too little leg and too much booty, a fat hairy arse and middle-aged spread, a short little shit: I was anything negative you cared to name. Why would Adrian find me attractive?

That night, as I lay in the bath, my little periscope breached the surface of the sudsy water. I had been thinking about Adrian again, thinking about our cuddle and how we had fit together. I wished I was as honest as Ben. He liked women but certain guys did it for him. I liked women, and didn't think I could feel anything for a guy and yet...there could be no denying it; I had been in love for months. Only now were my heads, both little and large, catching up with my heart.

As I lay there in the bath I caught the scent of cinnamon; that was always a good sign. Adrian was busy in the kitchen and I would be in for a treat. A few minutes later he knocked on the bathroom door. It was the first time ever he wanted to come into the bathroom while I was in there and I was in a panic; the blood drained from my naughty soldier. I wanted to put a flannel over my gonads but that seemed really silly somehow. This was, after all, the man that I would probably spend the rest of my life with.

'Come in.' I said.

He handed me a glass of red wine.

'I'm having one too.' he said. 'I thought you might like one. '

'It's a bit decadent.' I said.

'Yeah well, if I get drunk enough I won't think about how horny I am.'

I saw him look down at my cock and I realized that I was back on the bone. I quickly covered it with a flannel.

'Sorry, I don't know what's wrong with the damned thing.' I said.

He just laughed and left the room. I was mortified. Why on earth had my cock sprang up like that when he told me how horny he was feeling? I knew then that I was fighting a losing battle. And suddenly, I didn't care. The more I thought about it, the more I realized that I had nothing left to lose. I couldn't bear the thought of losing Adrian, not even for one night to some unknown stranger in a gay bar somewhere.

The meal was exceptional, probably the best that Adrian had ever prepared. But he was strangely quiet.

'Are you thinking about Ben?' I asked.

'A little.' he replied.

'Did you know that he was bi when you met him?'

He laughed.

'No. I thought he was totally straight. I was in the bar over at the hotel with a lady friend of mine and he kept on looking over. I thought he was into Jeanie but when I went to the bathroom he was suddenly standing next to me and stroking on a serious piece of meat.'

'Oh my! What did you do?' I asked.

'I did the only thing I could do...I took him into a cubicle.'

'You dirty slut!' I pretended to be annoyed.

He grinned.

'You've seen how small I am.' I said. 'I don't understand how you could be interested in someone like me.'

'It's not as if I have any choice in the matter.' he said. 'It was probably written in the stars a long, long time ago.'

It felt like electricity had surged through me. I wanted to smile and found it hard to keep a straight face, but I needed to for I needed to hear more. His words were like a drug flowing into my ears and into the pleasure receptors in my brain. None of the negative things that my ex had pointed out could affect us because this was something way beyond that. Just as my being straight was not enough of a hurdle, my looks, or rather lack of them, would prove no stumbling block. This really was something greater than us, something written in the stars, as Adrian said.

'Why didn't you ever say anything?'

'What was there to say? You were straight, I was gay; it seemed good fortune enough that you wanted to spend time with me. The last thing I wanted to do was tell you how I felt and scare you off.'

'So why have you told me now?'

'Because you won't let me out to play.' he gulped.

'I'm not just being possessive.' I said. 'There genuinely is stuffing going on inside my head that I don't know how to explain.'

'You don't have to say a word.'

'Just give me a little time, huh?' I said.

He winked and nodded.

That night Adrian and I shared a bed again and I held him in my arms all night long. It felt as wonderful as it did the night before, and he didn't put any pressure on me to do more than that. For the next six weeks we shared a bed every Friday night. I came to look forward to it; it was like a special treat to end the working week. We never again discussed him wanting to visit the city to get laid, or him seeing my hard cock in the bathroom. It was like we had reached a different level of understanding and I was really pleased about that.

And then, one Friday night, after we had been to a party, we were feeling a little tipsy. As I wrapped my arms around him I thought 'why shouldn't I?', so I slid my hand down his flat belly and onto his throbbing crotch. The rest, as they say, is history. We made love all night long, and in every position you can think of. I let him breach my defences, and I lay down my masculinity at his feet; I was rewarded with the most intense sensations and a feeling of total calm afterwards.

And now, I have perfect peace. I am in love with a man. So what? I kiss and cuddle and make love to Adrian and wild horses could not drag me away from his bed. I guess the guys at work were right all along!

***

Love Letters to His Ex

Dear Terry

Forgive me for getting in touch, though you asked me not to; you must have known that there is no way that I would not have written. I am made of sterner stuff than you may realize, and I do not give up without a fight. I know that you have to use this email address; I just hope that you won't delete my message without reading it. At least I can say that I have tried.

I just knew there was something wrong, when I pulled into the drive, last Friday night. Your car wasn't there, but there was nothing unusual in that. I know that sometimes you like to go have a beer with your buddies at the end of the week. However, there was something niggling away at me and as I let myself into the house my apprehension grew. A chill went down my spine, as though I had seen a ghost. And then when I went into the kitchen I saw your note.

I have to tell you that the shock was so great that I threw up. I've heard about people doing that and just assumed it was artistic licence used in books and films. How was I to know that nausea would engulf me like that? I only just made it to the bathroom on legs that felt as if they had been turned to jelly. I don't believe that I have ever felt so ill in my entire life. Afterwards, I reread your note, over and over, until at last the tears started to flow. A few stiff drinks later the pain had numbed enough for me to go to bed. But in the morning the pain was back again.

The cats are so confused by your absence. Every time they hear a car drive by they prick up their ears and look so disappointed that it's not you coming home to them. I try to give them cuddles for two, but it's not the same. They miss Dad number two.

How I got through the weekend I'll never know. I tried to imagine where you might be, and who with. I used to dread this day arriving but, as the years rolled, by I grew more and more confident and pushed it to the back of my mind. Four and a half years of happiness; surely that had to count for something? It was funny how in your leaving note you reminded me that you were straight when we first met. I've never forgotten that. It was not my intention to go falling in love with a straight guy but, once it happened, there was no holding back. I thought that I was headed for a lifetime of heartache, living all alone, and then you climbed into my bed one cold winter night and, it seems, we've never looked back.

I wonder how long it took you to compose your note. I know that you're not heartless and cruel but you might as well have ripped out my heart and fed it to a pack of wild dogs. You reminded me that you have always wanted children. Yes, I knew that but I pushed it to the back of my mind. I mean, there was no way it was going to happen...not with me, at any rate. And now suddenly you've met a woman that you want to be with, and start a family with. Talk about being dazed and confused! Where has this come from? Who is she? Where did you meet? How long have you known her?

I feel as if we have been living separate lives or that you have been living a secret life. How could I not have been aware of this? Were you sleeping with her while you were sleeping with me? We've always been able to talk about everything so how come this thing between you and her has been kept under wraps so completely? Did you think I would try to get you to change your mind if we discussed it? You bet I would. I'm hopping mad and what I really want if for you to jump in your vehicle and come on home.

We've spent every night together for the past four and a half years. Do you know what it feels like to suddenly be without you? Nothing makes sense anymore. The silence in the house threatens to engulf me. I miss your goofy grin and your big, hairy body. I miss your silly sense of humour and the way you attacked every meal I ever served you. You made me feel like the world's greatest chef! Lover, I'm going out of my mind with worry. Is this it between us? Are you really going to throw away four and a half years of laughter, companionship and love? Is this woman's hold on you so strong that you would cut me out of your life like this? It seems crazy to think that it has been less than a week since we last made love and now you are in someone else's bed.

People at work asked me what was wrong today and I had to lie and say I was feeling a bit under the weather. How can I tell them that the love of my life has walked out on me? I can still remember all the flak I took when we first got together. What right had I to go around seducing straight men, people wanted to know? I think the women thought I could not be trusted and the men were even more worried. If big Terry could graze on the other side of the fence what did it mean for them? I even had Pete come to see me to make me promise that I would never tell anyone about what had happened between us. I've never told you about Pete before, have I? A few too many beers and all the stuff he used to say, all the names he called me, just vanished.

Once people realized that we were serious their attitudes softened. There are actually a few of the ladies at work who think our romance is quite sweet. Well, it was sweet. I've lost the best thing that ever happened to me. So you see, Terry, I can't just let you go without at least trying to win you back. I'm appealing to all that is decent and human within you: don't abandon me like this.

I'm sorry to be so needy but where am I to find love again in a town as small as this. Besides Pete, there has been only a handful of others but they're all on the straight and narrow. None of these men have your courage. Once you had decided that I was the one for you there was no going back. You didn't give a damn about what people thought, or said, about you. Even your own family shunned you for a while but you didn't care.

Your Dad came to see me at work to ask if I knew where you were. He said they had had this strange phone call from you and you sounded distressed. I told him all I knew, and he apologized for what had happened. He's come a long way over the last four and a half years. He actually gave me a hug and said he was truly sorry about what had happened.

I was hurting, and I needed to lash out at someone.

'Aren't you pleased that maybe now you will have a grandchild?' I asked.

'Not if it means that you have to get hurt this way.' he said.

I just shrugged; trying to hold back the tears I could feel stinging my eyes.

'I know I said some hurtful things at the beginning.' he said to me. 'We were in shock. Our big, masculine son had suddenly announced that he was moving in with a gay guy. Terry, captain of the football team, and every girl's dream date was moving in with a guy. We couldn't understand it. But, over the years, we've come to see what a lovely man you are. We know that you would never do a thing to harm Terry and it was always obvious how happy you two were together.'

I smiled, weakly, and then it was time to say goodbye. What else was there to say? Perhaps a year from now, when you present his new grandchild to him, he might change his mind.

Oh I must have been crazy, thinking I could play happy families with a straight guy. Perhaps four and a half years is a pretty decent run and I've been living on borrowed time. I've seen your little stash of straight porn but didn't see the point in mentioning it. It was just a bit of harmless fun, I told myself. How deluded could I have been? For how long have you wanted to leave me? The thing that really confuses me is that it never felt like you were faking it in bed. Surely this can't be a sudden impulse. You didn't just wake up one day recently and think "I want kids" and go out and find a woman to run away with?

Well, I've said all the things I wanted to say. I'd like you to come home but I have a feeling that you will dig your heels in. Just as you resisted all attempts other people made to try and part us, I'm sure you will now not take any notice of anything I have to say. It seems that once you have made up your mind to do something wild horses couldn't drag you away.

So, I guess I'll just die a little with each passing day. I will sit clutching a whisky each evening as I remember the gorgeous hunk who once was mine. This is a fate worse than death and I beg you to change your mind. Try to remember all of the wonderful times that we had together.

You must know that I could never stop loving you.

Mack

Dear Terry

I'm guessing that either you deleted my message without reading it or you read it and don't want to reply. Either way, I hope that you will forgive me for having another go.

It doesn't feel right to give up too easily. For my own peace of mind I have to know that I at least tried. You don't just let your lover walk away from a wonderful relationship without so much as at least asking for a second chance. Whatever I've done to hurt you can be fixed. We can get over whatever I've done to make you stop believing in me.

I've always been tenacious. I used to cry through sheer frustration when I could get my sums right when I was young but I refused all help. I just stuck with it, over and over, until one day it clicked and I've never looked back since. I was always picked last for sporting teams in my early years at school and, at first, it turned me inward. I thought "I can't be bothered with them if they can't be bothered with me". But it did bother me and so I toughened myself up and learned the rules. I can't say that I ever became a first class sportsman but I made myself useful.

I've taught myself to do so many different things because I don't like having to rely on anyone else. I can cook, bake, sew, unblock a drain and service my vehicle. I remember once the office jock's engine wouldn't start and I sorted it out for him. He had been peering under the hood for ages but knew that he hadn't a clue. He was desperately embarrassed, especially because he had called me some really nasty names when we were back in high school.

'But you're gay, right?' he asked when I had got his engine running.

'What's that got to do with anything?' I asked.

'Well, I just thought...'

'That I couldn't handle anything mechanical?' I asked.

'Well, it's just...'

At least he had the sense to realize that he was in a hole and that he should stop digging. He offered to buy me a beer and it was a rather awkward affair. He had one eye on the door; I guess he was hoping that no one he knew would come into that bar and see him drinking with a gay guy. I've never found him attractive, though many do; his arrogance scars his pretty features. I'm not sure which one of us wanted to get out of there most; I think he might have been impressed with how quickly I knocked back my beer!

All of these things I learned because I did not want to be beholden to anyone. And then you came along and taught me that it was ok to love, that it was ok not to keep a tight reign on my heart. I realized, through your example that you have to take a chance if you want to be happy. And oh, we were happy! I was happier than I've ever been in my life before. I took a chance on love and now I'm taking another chance; if there is any way that our relationship can be salvaged then we should do that.

You've asked me to let you go and I don't want to be beholden to you, but I am. I need you. My life without you is bleak. The emptiness hangs in this house and haunts me. I try to pretend that you've just gone away for a while. I tell myself that soon I will hear your tyres crunching the gravel in the drive. Kodi and Kara will prick up their ears and know that you've come back to them. But, it doesn't happen; another day passes without you.

Please contact me. I couldn't bear it if things ended between us in this cold way. We've shared too much for that to happen.

Love

Mack

Dear Mack

I knew that you would contact me and there is no way that I could have deleted your message without reading it.

I know that what I have done to you is deeply hurtful but please let me explain. That first time I went to bed with you I didn't think too much about it. I mean, every straight guy gets to slip up at least once in his life, right. It was no big deal: I'd made love to a guy, so what? You see, I've always had this ideal in my head that I would settle down with a woman and raise a family. That's what people do. That's what my Dad did, and Pops before him and all of his ancestors before him. At least, as far as I know. Who knows, there may have been a man in the family lusting up on another man but, if there was, he put duty before pleasure or else I wouldn't be here now.

Even after the second and third time we made love I wasn't too worried. It was just a little blip; I was still basically a straight guy. But then I fell in love with you, and moved in with you and I watched the dream slip further and further away from me. Not too long ago Rob showed me a picture of his new born son. He was as proud as can be and I felt about two inches tall. Something happened to me that day; things started to unravel. This happy little life that I had built with you could not give me the joy that I saw shining in Rob's eyes.

Raine is not someone that I had just met. I knew her years ago, before I met you. We went out together for a while but then she broke up with me for another guy. I was devastated and heart-broken. It was a relief when she moved away as I didn't have to see her and be reminded of how she had hurt me. And then, just recently, I saw her in town. She had come back to visit a friend. We got chatting and she told me that letting me go was the worst mistake she had ever made in her life. One thing led to another and I told her how I felt I had missed out by not being a father.

'Come away with me.' Raine said.

'I can't. I replied. 'I can't do that to Mack.'

'This is our last chance.' Raine replied. 'We can go back to how it was before. We can start a family. Be brave.'

I don't feel very brave. I knew that if you and I had discussed what I was feeling you would have talked me out of leaving. I really felt like this was my last chance to get back to the dream. I'm not brave. I am a coward, and I took the coward's way out. So here I am living with a woman I feel I hardly know. And I can't stop thinking about how I did you wrong.

I thought I'd be happy, you know? Here I was going back in time, stepping beyond the rainbow with my first true love. And all I am is scared. We've both changed, Raine and I. Anyway, I've made this bed so I've got to lie in it.

Baby, I'm asking you a favour; please let me go. I know that you love me. I doubt that Raine ever loved me as much as you do and, deep down, I know that she can't, but you've got to let me go. I've given up so much to be where I am now. I just need to knuckle down and make this thing work out for Raine and me.

I hope that you meet someone else. I know how much love you have to give and you are a sweet, lovely guy. You deserve so much more than me. You need a man who is into men. You need a man who would run for his life at the thought of making babies with a woman!

Don't hate me too much.

Terry

Dear Terry

I could never hate you. I have loved you from the moment I first set eyes on you in the hotel bar. Of course, that evening, you only had eyes for Darla. My poor, sweet lesbian friend was a little confused. She thought you were buying us drinks because you wanted to get into my pants! I was smitten with you. Your manners were so impeccable and those big, blue eyes of yours looked so full of vitality.

I hung on every word you said as I dreamed about kissing those full, red lips of yours and stroking the stubble on your cheeks. When you touched my shoulder I swore I felt a spark but that must have been my imagination. I laughed at all of your jokes and thought that if I were a lesbian I would go bi for you. I could see that you were a little confused when we got up to leave. Your charm had failed to get you what you wanted. You must have sussed that I was gay, so that couldn't have been the problem. What you hadn't figured out was that Darla was gay too.

When I ran into you a couple of weeks later you asked about Darla and I told you that she was gay.

'Well, I never!' you replied. 'I knew that you were gay but I had no idea that she was.'

'How did you know I'm gay?' I replied.

'You about stripped my clothes off with those hungry eyes of yours.' you replied.

I blushed and squirmed.

'Do you want to go get a beer?' you asked. 'My ego is pretty low at the moment; I could do with spending time with someone like you.'

How was I to know what that one beer would lead to? Soon you were coming round to my house every Friday night and I was falling deeper and deeper under your spell. When I told you that I thought I should stop seeing you because I was falling in love your answer was hop into bed with me. I floated somewhere beyond the stars that night. I had never experienced such joy and ecstasy. I knew that this was a one-off but I was determined to enjoy it all the same. When I awoke, and found that I was still snuggled in your arms, I dared to dream that maybe this time I would get lucky.

Living in a small town has its rewards but not so much when it comes to finding love. There have been men, older men whose love-life has waned, who have stepped out of the shadows a few times to have a little naughty fun with me. But that's all it was: fun. There was no way they wanted to be in a relationship with a guy. But you were different. You came back, after that first time and you stayed the night again. And in the morning I thought surely this is when I get the goodbye speech. But you came back again, and again. Before too long I could relax, safe in the knowledge that you were mine.

It was the craziest situation, I have to admit. People I thought were friends were all telling me to end the madness, and give you up. What they didn't know is that you had no intention of going anywhere. Those first few months were sheer heaven on earth. The more you opened up, the more you fell in love. Finally I had what I had been longing for all of my adult life. A man of my own! You weren't somebody's husband; you weren't just out for a quickie on a Saturday afternoon.

And now, my love, you have left me. You walked out of my life just as quickly as you came into it. I have to grant you that; you don't do things by halves. It's all or nothing with you. If I were reading a book, or watching a movie, I would find this a most interesting story. But it's happening to me and it's my heart that's breaking. How could fate have been so cruel to me?

I'm going to do what you ask: I'm going to let you go. But there is one thing you need to know: I will always love you. If you ever find that you want to come back to me, for whatever reason, my door will always be open.

My bed is too big without you.

Love

Mack

Dear Mack

Sorry that is has taken me two months to get back to you. Something has happened and you are the only person that I can talk to. I'm sorry if that seems callous but I've got to get this off my chest.

I've been really trying to make things work with Raine. The way we've been carrying on I thought she would be pregnant by now. She keeps reminding me that the clock is ticking and I feel like I'm just part of some master plan. I've been bending over backwards to accommodate her quirks and demands. I know, I know...I chose this. But this isn't what I need to tell you about.

I was feeling really pressurized recently and I rebelled by going to a bar instead of going home from work. As soon as I stepped into that bar I knew what kind of place it was. I swear it was a genuine mistake, but I could have chosen to leave and I didn't. This businessman started chatting to me and asked if he could buy me a beer. Oh, I knew what he wanted. It was right there in his eyes, just like it was with you. I should have resisted, but I didn't. We went to a cheap hotel and I let him have me in a way that I thought only you ever would.

I feel so ashamed. I feel as though I've cheated on you and Raine. Does that make any sense? Why can't the course of my life run smooth? Why do I need to be on this roller coaster of emotions, falling for a gay guy then bailing out on him for an ex-girlfriend and now unable to decide which of them I've wronged most? And why, oh why, did I enjoy what that stranger and I did in that rented-by-the-hour bed?

I left one dead-end job for another, and it shouldn't make any difference but it does. I'm bored and unhappy at work. I'm on edge and stressed at home. And I snuck out to be with a guy. Am I just looking at life through rose-tinted glasses? Do I need a family to be happy, I wonder. I thought I was doing fine; I thought I was getting over you and then as soon as I was in that man's arms I knew I was lying to myself.

Mack, what would you do if you were in my shoes? No wait, you're the sensible one. You would never have had your head turned by an ex showing up out of the blue. You would never have left, I know. I'm so sad right now, and I just want you to know.

Love

Terry

Dear Terry

Well, I must say that I was surprised by your news. Here you were, back at the top table again. You had bought a one-way ticket on the heterosexual train; you were bound for conventional happiness yet you decided to derail those grand plans. How long will it be before you are back in that bar? And it is not even me that's to blame this time.

I, too, have been with someone. Nick is the new barman at the hotel. I'm not sure about him, somehow. It was fun and it was physical but I don't feel comfortable with him. I just can't put my finger on it. He is a drifter, so it wouldn't be sensible me hanging my hopes on him. I'm too comfortable in this little town to ever leave. Or is that too cowardly? I've seen Nick a couple of times but I just don't know where this is going and, to be honest, I just wish that he would up and leave. While he is here the temptation to get it together with him is too strong but when I'm in his bed I can't wait to leave.

Yours

Mack

Dear Mack

When I read your letter it felt like someone had punched me in the gut. I didn't think that you would get over me so quickly.

Raine has cast aspersions upon the quality of my little swimmers. She said she felt that she ought to be pregnant after over three months of trying. I told her that I wanted to ease up on all the lovemaking and she accused me of having a lover. If only! What a mess this is turning out to be. The sweet, funny, spontaneous girl I knew all those years ago has changed into a somewhat hard and scheming woman. I think she knows that getting back with me was a mistake. We're both too proud to admit it.

Oh, I'm so jealous of you and that barman. If he makes you feel so uncomfortable should you not stop seeing him? And that's not just the green-eyed monster talking. I care about you and I want you to be happy.

I've changed jobs and I'm hoping that things will be a little different in this new job. It's too much to be unhappy at work and at home. I'm sure this can't be the best environment for conception. I'm stressed and Raine's stressed. I'm not quite sure why she is so desperate to get pregnant. Perhaps she feels that if I become a father I will put you behind a barrier where you can't be recalled. Apparently I called out your name in my sleep recently and that lead to a huge argument between us. I've never lied to her. I told her right from the start what you meant to me and she suggested that we could have something grander than that. They say you should never go back and maybe it's true.

What was I thinking, buddy? How could I have walked away from a four and a half year relationship with a man and think I could just pick up my straight life where I left off? I dream about men in my sleep; I hunger for a man's touch. I feel like I'm not trying hard enough with Raine but I don't know how to do more. If she didn't pressurize me about getting her pregnant things might have been different between us although, in all honesty, I'm not sure that they would be.

I know that I asked you to let me go but please think about me sometimes. I feel so lost and alone here in the city. I don't belong in an environment like this and I feel on edge all the time. Think about me now and then. And remember me to Kodi and Kara.

Love

Terry

Dear Terry

You big oaf! I think about you all the time. I'm even afraid to think about you too much in case it weirds you out. I know that Kodi and Kara think about you too. I often find them curled up together in your armchair and that is not something they used to do before.

Things came to a head between me and Nick when he stole some money out of my wallet. I confronted him and of course he denied it but I knew how much was in there to start with. He went off in a huff and said he never wanted to see me again and all I felt was relief. I'd rather be alone than feel so uncomfortable with a lover.

The whole pregnancy thing with Raine must be a little difficult to cope with, but isn't it what you wanted. You said you've always wanted a family and now is your chance. This is something I could never give you, not even with adopted kids. I'm just not into the whole 'happy families' thing. Two is enough to make me happy. Just us is all I ever had to offer you. What a shame that it was not enough.

How is the new job working out? You're right, life is too short to be unhappy both at home and at work. Now that you've left me, and I'm done with Nick, I have time on my hands and may look into studying again. I did a couple of long distance courses in the past and found that I really enjoyed them. I'm not saying that you prevented me studying but I was simply too content while living with you to think about studying. I've also been hanging out with Melody again. We used to hang out a bit before you and I hooked up. She recently broke up with Jordi so she is at a loose end too. She is talking about moving away but I know that she and Jordi were meant to be together.

Well, that's about all the news that I have to share. I hope that things improve between you and Raine. Only you know how much you want this to work out. If you can get over the teething troubles in your relationship you might be rewarded with being a father. You have told me how much this means to you so my advice would be to go the extra mile to get what you want.

Yours

Mack

Dear Mack

Only 'yours' huh? No more love? I guess I don't deserve it, but I still think very fondly of you.

Raine is still not pregnant and she is talking about us seeking medical help. I think the only one who needs help is me. What was I thinking? I got really stressed out and went back to that bar I told you about and ended up going home with a guy. This is really messed up isn't it? I think I'm going to have to tell Raine this isn't working. It's unfair to her for me to be behaving like this.

I've been thinking long and hard about having kids and I've decided maybe that isn't what I want anymore. Or, maybe I don't want it enough. I'm not sad that Raine isn't pregnant and I'm beginning to think that I would be upset if she did get pregnant. I've got to end this, haven't I? Mack, please tell me what to do. I walked into this with my eyes wide open but I feel like I'm drowning now.

I can just see you hitting the books! I have to say that I am glad you are no longer involved with Nick. I know it's silly, but that's just the way I feel.

I'm not enjoying my new job any more than I did the old. I think the problem is that there is too much other stuff going on in my life right now. I miss home. I miss you. I miss Kodi and Kara. I miss hearing their little purrs. When I suggested to Raine that we get a cat she said there was no way she would allow an animal in the apartment. I think I knew then that we were doomed. Where did she go, that beautiful girl I used to know? Or, is it just that I have changed. If I'm still sleeping with guys there must be a reason for that. I used to see my self as a straight guy that just happened to be in love with a gay guy. Now I see myself as a straight guy who is wallowing in a crock of shit.

Mack, you've always been the stronger of the two of us. Tell me what to do. I can't go on like this.

Love

Terry

Dear Terry

It makes me sad that you are so sad but it is unfair to ask me to tell you what to do. You know what my answer would be.

I've had to go back to sneaking around with married men, and I don't like that. While I've been off the scene the little network has grown. I've been introduced to half a dozen guys who are all on the prowl, from time to time. I get so lonely, and so horny, that I drive myself crazy. I tell myself that I'm just going down to the Post Office to check my mailbox at nine o'clock on a Friday night but really I know what I'm hoping to find along the way. I thought that I had moved on from this. To be right back where I started feels like failure. Perhaps I really do need to start to think about moving away from this place.

Nick has moved on. He stole some money from the till and Bert gave him the boot. It turns out that he has left a little memento behind. Rita is pregnant by him. And city folk think that nothing ever happens in Hicksville!

I'm thinking about taking a writing course. I have had so many mixed emotions over the last few months that I feel it would help by writing them down. Don't worry; I'll change your name if I ever write about us. I don't think many people would believe our story anyway. They would probably just say that it was wishful thinking on my part that I could get a straight guy to fall in love with me.

Here's a little something that I wrote:

And the gleam
That I thought was gold
Turned out just to be rust
Catching the light right
And the dream
That I was sold
Turned out to be faulty
There was no you and me
No, I was all alone
Without a money-back guarantee

I saw your Dad recently and he said that he was really worried that they had heard so little from you. I lied and said that you were fine. What would he say if he knew that you were just being used as a baby making machine? Just kidding! You ought to get in touch with your folk. I know that you were always close and it must be breaking their hearts that you are keeping your distance now. There is no need to feel ashamed. We all make mistakes. You chased after your dream and you couldn't have known that it wouldn't work out the way you wanted it to. People change; you can't expect Raine to be the girl you once knew and you can't hate her for having changed. Perhaps you might be happier with a different woman, one you were more compatible with? If you found someone new, and took things easy, perhaps the dream of being a family man could still be on track.

It's late, and I'm tired and a little drunk. I had better end this before I say things that I might regret later.

Look after yourself.

Love

Mack

Dear Mack

Well, I've found the solution to at least one of my problems. Raine was nagging at me about us seeking medical help to get her pregnant and I just snapped. I told her that I didn't want to have anyone poking about in my underpants and that I didn't want to make love to her any more. She went mental and told me to get out of her apartment, and out of her life. I tried to reason with her but she was having none of it. I realized then that I never really knew her at all.

As usual, you were right. She has changed and it isn't fair of me to expect her not to have. This whole thing has left a nasty taste in my mouth but I'm so relieved that it is over.

I'm holed up in a cheap hotel while I try to figure out what to do with my life. I've too much time on my hands and, though I'm relieved that it's over with Raine, I still get depressed when I try to figure out what went wrong. It doesn't help that the gay bar is just a five minute walk from here and I keep finding myself being weak. Half an hour of pleasure leads to days of guilt and shame. Not because I slept with a man, you understand, but because I threw away the best thing I ever had.

The impulsive decision to run away with Raine is beginning to look more and more like the worst one I have ever made. It feels as though I had been looking at her through gauze. I couldn't connect. I couldn't find the pathway back to her heart and I feel like such a failure. Was it me, or was it her? I guess I will never know. However, one thing that I do know is I'm glad it's over.

I've not had a decent night's sleep since I got here. The guy in the room on one side of me is a rowdy alcoholic and the woman in the room on the other side of me is on the game. All night long there are people coming and going and these strange noises being made and no, I'm not talking about those kinds of noises either. Add those in, and it's enough to kill anyone's libido and swear you off drink for the rest of your life! Seriously though, this place is the pits and the sooner I get out of here the better.

I guess you will sleep easier at night knowing that Nick is no longer around. That bad boy must have had a whole lot of charm, though! He is probably drifting across the planes as we speak, thinking about where to call in next.

I've not been in touch with my parents because I know that they would not be happy with the choices I have made lately. They tried to talk me out of moving in with you but, to their credit, once they got over the shock they were very supportive. It shows how much you mean to them that they still talk to you even though we are no longer together. Give them my regards and tell them I will write soon.

You said some things in your letter which I didn't really understand. Am I being thick or do you still have feelings for me? I know that would be asking too much after the way I have treated you. I don't know that hooking up with another woman is going to make too much difference. I'm beginning to see now that that was all a pipe dream. I miss the ease of being with a man. Raine always wanted me to be paying attention to her and I just couldn't do it. If I sat down and read a newspaper she thought I was ignoring her.

I wish that you weren't so far away from me. I'd love to sit down and talk to you and see your handsome face again. I could always see the love shining in your eyes. I think perhaps you have spoilt me for all time. For four and a half years I thought I was royalty and now I discover that I'm just an ordinary man...an ordinary man who has lost his way. I think it is time to stop running away from whom and what I am. I am a man who has the capacity to love another man deeply and completely. What a fool I have been.

There's something I want you to know. I know that lately I have been behaving like a slut but in all the time we were together I never once cheated on you. Not with a man, or a woman. I don't know if that counts for anything but I just need you to know that.

Love

Terry

Dear Terry

Firstly, let me say that I am sorry that things have ended this way between you and Raine. It never is easy letting go of a dream. I find her behaviour odd so it must be even more perplexing for you. But then again, what was she to make of the fact that you had been in a relationship with a man for four and a half years? Perhaps too much water had passed under the bridge and that water was too muddy to see through.

We have both made mistakes. I was too proud to say what you wanted to hear. Not any more...come on home. I love you and I miss you and we belong together. You can screw every single man in that bar and it will never amount to a hill of beans. You love me; I know that and you know that. You can chase around the world all you want to, nothing is going to change the fact that you belong to me.

Come on home. The cats are getting restless with waiting for you to return. I'm getting bored with these duplicitous middle-aged men who inhabit my world. I'd like to cast them out and tell them that my prince has returned.

There is no point both of us being unhappy when we are so very good at making each other happy. Check out of that flea pit of a hotel and come and take your rightful place at my side.

I was right about Melody and Jordi; they have got back together so I am at a loose end over here. I need someone warm and cuddly to help me out. OK. OK, I'm no longer asking; I'm telling you what to do, just like you asked me to.

Come home!

Love

Mack

Dear Mack

I am trembling with excitement. My bags are packed and I'm going to check out of the hotel within the next five minutes and start driving.

I should be home at dawn. Have a big breakfast waiting for me and tell Kodi and Kara that I'm a coming home!

Love you loads.

Terry

Dear Terry

I know that you won't read this until you are already back home with me but I just wanted you to know that you mean the world to me. I could never love anyone else as much as I love you and I'm glad that you have come to your senses.

I've told Kodi and Kara that Dad number two will be home soon.

Love you more than you will ever know.

Mack

***

Printed in Poland
by Amazon Fulfillment
Poland Sp. z o.o., Wrocław